11/8

D0438396

Let Sleeping Dragons Lie

Let Sleeping Dragons Lie

Garth Nix
&
Sean Williams

SCHOLASTIC PRESS · NEW YORK

To Anna, Thomas, Edward,
and all my family and friends.
— Garth Nix

To Amanda, and all our friends and
family, with gratitude and love.
— Sean Williams

Bilewolves!"

"Help us!"

"Help me!"

"Aarrgh, no, no —"

The shouts and screams grew louder as Sir Odo and Sir Eleanor raced toward the village green, their magical, self-willed swords, Biter and Runnel, almost lifting them from the ground in their own eagerness to join the combat. Well behind them came Addyson and Aaric, the baker's twin boys, who had come in a panic to tell them the village was under attack.

Above all the human sounds of fear and fighting, a terrible howling came again, from more than one bestial throat.

"Slower!" panted Odo as they reached the back of the village inn, the Sign of the Silver Fleece, or the Gray Sheep, as it was nicknamed, since the sign had long since faded. "We must be clever. Stay shoulder to shoulder, advance with care."

"Nay, we must charge at once!" roared Biter, even as his sister sword snapped, "I agree, Sir Odo."

"I do too," said Eleanor, slowing so her much larger and less fleet-of-foot friend could catch up. When he was level with her, she moved closer so they were indeed shoulder to shoulder, their swords held in the guard position.

Together, and ready, they rounded the corner of the inn.

A terrible scene met their eyes. Some forty paces away, four enormous, shaggy, wolflike creatures, each the size of a small horse, stood at bay opposite a man and a woman. The people were hunters or trappers, judging by their leather armor and well-traveled boots, although they were quite old to be in that trade. Both looked to be at least fifty.

The man had a cloth of shining gold tied around his eyes, which perhaps explained Addyson's panicked description of "a blind king" being attacked by the bilewolves. The cloth *did* give the impression of a crown.

Blind or not, king or not, the man wielded his steel-shod staff with a brilliance that made Odo gasp. The weapon was a blur, leaping out to punch one bilewolf's snout, then jab another's forefoot. The woman was equally as adept, though she wielded a curved sword, the blade moving swiftly and smoothly as she danced with it, the bilewolves slow and clumsy partners. Close to the inn on the edge of the green, three villagers lay dead or seriously wounded, their torn and jagged clothes still smoking from the bilewolves' acid-spewing jaws. Eleanor's father, the herbalist Symon, was bent over the closest victim, frantically trying to stem the flow of blood from a wound. He looked up for a second at his daughter, but did not speak, turning instantly back to his work.

Odo grasped the situation immediately. Only the two old warriors kept the bilewolves away from the wounded and the rest of the defenseless villagers. But the two were outnumbered and, despite their skill, overmatched by the sheer size and ferocity of the animals.

"Forward!" Odo shouted, and he and Eleanor marched together.

"For Lenburh!" shouted Eleanor.

Odo knew from the slightest tremor in Eleanor's voice that she was afraid, though no one else would be able to tell. He was afraid as well. They were only twelve years old and had been knights for little over a month, but he knew the fear would not stop Eleanor, and it wouldn't stop him either.

They did not expect their war cries to be answered, but off to the right came a shout: "Forward for Lenburh!" A horse came galloping across the green, the ancient warhorse of Sir Halfdan, who, like the master who rode it, had not been in battle for twenty years or more. True to its training, the warhorse held straight for the bilewolves, despite their terrible stench and formidable snarls. Sir Halfdan, despite age and infirmity, was rock-solid in the saddle, a lance couched under his arm. He had not had time to put on any armor save his helmet and a gauntlet. He still wore the nightgown that was his usual garb these days, and his one foot was still clad in a velvet slipper.

A bilewolf turned towards the galloping horse and charged, leaping at the last moment to avoid Sir Halfdan's lowering lance. But the old knight knew that trick and flicked the point up, taking the beast in the shoulder, the steel point punching deep. Bilewolf shrieked, the lance snapped, and then horse, knight, and dying bilewolf collided and went flying.

At the same time, one of the three remaining bilewolves bounded up on the back of one of its fellows and leaped high over the head of the blind staff-wielder. The man jumped upon his companion's shoulders and punched up at the bilewolf's belly, but the beast had launched itself too well. The staff merely struck its wiry tail, severing it midway along as the bilewolf flew past them.

Odo and Eleanor rushed across the green, expecting the falling bilewolf to attack them and the unprotected villagers behind. But it ignored them, spinning about as it landed to strike at the two warriors once again, dark blood spraying from its injured tail. The blind man jumped down with the deftness of a traveling acrobat and stood back-to-back with the woman. Together they turned in a circle, staff and sword blurring to hold the bilewolves at bay.

Odo slowed and edged cautiously closer, wondering how the blindfolded man had struck so precisely with his staff. Meanwhile, Eleanor narrowed her eyes, seeking a way into the battle.

"Take the one to my right!" shouted the swordswoman to Odo and Eleanor, her voice strong and well used to command. "It is already lamed!"

"Sixth and Fourth Stance!" said Eleanor. "You high, me low."

They moved in perfect synchrony, as they'd practiced, Odo stepping left and out, Biter held above his head to strike in a slanting downwards blow, as Eleanor stretched out low with a lunge at the bilewolf's right front leg, which it already favored.

The bilewolf bunched itself to leap up at Odo, choosing the bigger target. But Runnel's sharp point cut through its leg even as it sprang. It fell sideways, yelping, and Biter came down to separate its massive head from its body, the sword twisting to avoid a spray of bile from the snapping jaws. Both young knights struck again to be sure it was dead, and then swung about to move to the next target.

But the remaining two bilewolves were already slain, one with a crushed skull and the other with a sliced-open throat. All four carcasses lay steaming, the grass beneath them turning black and smoking where the acidic drops fell from their jaws.

"Sir Halfdan!" cried Eleanor. The old knight lay motionless upon the ground, the haft of his broken lance still couched under his arm. His warhorse lay near him, unable to get up. It raised its head and whinnied, as if in answer to some trumpet no one else could hear, but the effort was too much. Its head fell heavily back and did not move again.

"Wait!" Odo called as Eleanor started towards the old knight. "Do you see any more bilewolves?"

The swordswoman answered him. She and the man still stood back-to-back, their weapons ready, as if they expected another attack at any moment.

Or they didn't trust Odo and Eleanor.

"There will be none," she said. "They hunt in fours and are jealous of their prey. You are knights of the realm?"

"Uh, we're knights, but not . . . exactly of the realm, I don't think," said Odo. "I am Sir Odo."

"And I, Sir Eleanor." It gave her a small thrill to say that, although there were more pressing matters to consider. "If there are no more bilewolves, we must help Sir Halfdan while my father attends to the others —"

"One moment, Sir Eleanor," snapped the woman. "How are you knights, but *not exactly of the realm?*"

"It's a long story," said Odo. "We were knighted by the dragon Quenwulf —"

"Quenwulf?" asked the woman. Her expression shifted to one minutely more relaxed. "Was it she who gifted you with the enchanted swords you bear?"

"𝔑o!" said Biter. He was still not entirely convinced he shouldn't be a dragonslaying sword.

"Uh, no," said Odo. "We found them. Like I said, it is a long story —"

"Best saved for later," said the blind man. His voice was even more used to command than the woman's. "Take me to the fallen knight, Hundred. Sir Eleanor, did you say he was Sir Halfdan?"

"Yes, Sir Halfdan holds the manor here," Eleanor told the man as she studied the woman more closely. *Hundred* was a very strange name, but perhaps it was apt for a very strange person. In addition to the curved sword she still held at the ready, Eleanor noticed she had a series of small knives sheathed along each forearm, and unusual pouches on her belt. The backs of her dark-skinned hands were

white with dozens of scars, like Eleanor's mother's hands —
not wounds from claws or teeth, but weapon marks. A sign
of many years of combat and practice.

"Sir, we should go on at once," protested Hundred.

"No," said the man. He turned to face where Sir
Halfdan lay and began to walk towards him, using his
staff to tap the ground. After a moment, Hundred went
ahead of him, and the man stopped tapping and followed
her footfalls.

"He must have amazing hearing," whispered Eleanor
to Odo.

"I have *well-trained* ears," said the man without turning his head.

Odo and Eleanor exchanged glances, then hurried
after the odd duo.

Sir Halfdan lay on his back, not moving. His helmet,
too big for him, had tipped forward over his face. Hundred
knelt by his side and gently removed it. The old knight's
eyes opened as she did so, surprising everyone, for he had
seemed already dead.

"Sir Halfdan," said the blind man, bending over him.

Sir Halfdan blinked rheumily, and his jaw fell.

"Sire," he whispered. "Can it be?"

The old knight tried to lift his head and arm, but
could not do so. The blind man knelt by him and closed
his own hand over Halfdan's gauntlet.

"I remember when you held the bridge at Holmfirth,"
said the blind man. "In the second year of my reign. None
so brave as Sir Halfdan. You remember the song Veran
wrote? She will have to write another verse."

"That was long ago," whispered Halfdan.

"Time has no dominion over the brave."

"I thought . . . we thought you dead, sire."

Eleanor mouthed "sire" at Odo and hitched one shoulder in question. He shrugged, unable to explain what was going on. But looking at the blind man in profile, there was something familiar about the shape of his face, that beaky nose, the set chin.

"I gave up the throne," said the man. He touched his golden blindfold. "When I lost my sight, I thought I could no longer rule. I was wrong. Blindness makes a man a fool no more than a crown makes him king."

At the word *king*, Odo suddenly remembered why the old man's profile looked familiar.

It was on the old silver pennies he counted at the mill.

Eleanor had the same realization. They both sank together to the earth, their hauberks jangling. Odo went down on his right knee and Eleanor on her left. They looked at each other worriedly and started to spring up again to change knees, before Hundred glared at them and made a sign to be still.

"My time is done, sire," said Sir Halfdan. There was a rattle in his voice. He glanced over at his horse. "Old Thunderer has gone ahead, and I must follow . . ."

He paused for a moment, the effort of gathering his thoughts, of speaking, evident on his face.

"I commend to you, sire . . . two most brave knights . . . Sir Eleanor and Sir Odo. They —"

Whatever he was going to say next was lost. At that moment old Sir Halfdan died. Egda the First — for the blind man was certainly the former king of Tofte, who had abdicated ten years ago — gripped Sir Halfdan's shoulder in farewell and stood up, turning towards the kneeling Odo and Eleanor.

"He was a great and noble knight," he said. "The Hero of Holmfirth Bridge, and even then he must have been over forty. To think of him slaying a bilewolf at the age of ninety!"

"We didn't know he was a hero," said Eleanor uncomfortably. She was thinking about some of the names she had called him because he was slow getting organized for their journey east, to be introduced to the royal court. And how some people in the village had mocked him behind his back for having only one foot, though they would never dare do so to his face. "He was just our knight. He's been here so long . . . um . . . sorry, should I say 'sire,' or is it 'Your Highness'?"

"I am not a king," said the blind man. "I have been simply Egda these last ten years."

"*Sir* Egda," said Hundred sharply. "You may refer to his grace as 'sir' or 'sire.'"

"Now, now, Hundred," said Egda. He smiled faintly, exposing two rows of white, even teeth. "Hundred was the captain of my guard and has certain ideas about maintaining my former station. I wish to hear how you were made knights by the dragon Quenwulf, but first there is work to be done. The bilewolves must be burned. Are the

9

wounded villagers attended to? I hear pain, but also gentle soothing."

Eleanor looked over to where the wounded were now being lifted to be carried inside the inn. Her father was assisted by several other villagers, including the midwife Rowena, who often worked with him.

"They are being tended to by my father, who is a healer and herbalist, sir," she said.

"I'll gather wood to burn the bilewolves," said Odo. "Addyson and Aaric can help, if it please you, sir."

"I do not command here," said Egda mildly. "Who is Sir Halfdan's heir? Has he a daughter or son to take up his lands and sword? Or, given his age, grandchildren, perhaps?"

"There's no one," said Eleanor, frowning. She looked across at where the wounded or dead were being taken into the inn. "Only his squire, Bordan, and I think he was one of the three other people the bilewolves —"

"They sought to help us," said Egda. "Would that they were less brave."

"I warned them away," said Hundred harshly. "If they had kept back, they would have been in no danger."

"Only if the bilewolves were after you in *particular*," said Odo, made curious by her comment.

"This is not a matter for you, boy," said Hundred. "Sire, we must be on our —"

"No," interrupted the former king. He didn't seem happy with the way Hundred was addressing Odo's inquiries. "We will rest here tonight, not camp in the wilds. Sir

Halfdan was my father's knight before he served me. We must show proper respect, see him put to rest. Also, I want to hear the story of these two swords — who are strangely quiet now, though I heard them in the battle."

"I merely wait for my knight to introduce me, sir," said Biter. He sounded aggrieved. "He is new to his estate and I am still teaching him manners."

"Oh," said Odo. He held up Biter, hilt first. "This is Hildebrand Shining Foebiter. Often called Biter."

"And my sword is Reynfrida Sharp-point Flamecutter, or Runnel for short," said Eleanor.

"Greetings, sir," said Runnel.

"And welcome, sire," added Biter, not wanting to be left out.

Egda nodded. "Well then. Sir Odo, to the burning of the beasts. Sir Eleanor, if you would introduce me to your father and other notables in the village, we must order . . . that is, *suggest* the arrangements to lay Sir Halfdan to rest. Hundred, cast about for any sign of other unfriendly beasts."

"Sire!" protested Hundred. "I cannot leave you unprotected."

"Sir Eleanor, would you give me your arm?" asked Egda. "Sir Odo, would you take care to listen and come should I call for aid?"

"Yes, sir!" said Odo and Eleanor together.

"You see," said Egda to the frowning Hundred. "I have two knights to guard me. Come, let us be about our business!"

He strode off confidently towards the inn, tapping once more with his staff and hardly holding Eleanor's crooked arm at all. Odo stared after him. When he looked back to see what Hundred was doing, he was surprised to find himself alone. In just a few seconds, the elderly warrior had disappeared from the middle of the green!

Sire, the good villagers of Lenburh are assembled."

Hundred's soft voice broke the breath that Eleanor had been holding as she waited for Sir Halfdan's burial rites to begin. The elderly knight's body had rested all night in the manor house's great hall, wrapped in his best cloak with his shield across his chest and his sword at his side. Eleanor had volunteered to sit with him, and Odo had joined her, relieving her at the old knight's side when she grew tired. The two times she slept, she dreamed of her mother, who had once lain in that very spot. It seemed an age ago.

Now it was Sir Halfdan's turn. Reeve Gorbold relinquished his position at the head of the funerary procession to Sir Egda and joined the others bearing the body. Even though he was already one of the strongest villagers in Lenburh, Odo suppressed a grunt of effort as they raised Sir Halfdan high. What the old knight had lacked in a complete set of legs he had more than made up for in girth.

A lonely bell tolled as the solemn procession made down the hill to Sir Halfdan's family crypt, past the small fenced-off area of the estate where Eleanor's mother was buried.

Eleanor wondered if she would join her mother there one day. Someone would need to assume the mantle of Sir Halfdan's estate, and Odo was the most likely to settle here when he attained his majority. Eleanor herself would prefer to be adventuring and seeing the world.

Deep in these thoughts, Eleanor walked into Hundred's back as the procession came to a halt. The bodyguard clicked her tongue.

"Brave in heart," said Sir Egda, tapping one end of his staff softly against the earth, "and noble in death, we farewell this good knight and remember his deeds."

He stood aside to let Sir Halfdan's bearers into the darkness of the crypt itself, to the stone plinth that had long ago been prepared by Borden, Sir Halfdan's loyal squire, who had gone to his own grave earlier that day. Odo stooped to avoid banging his head, and tried to ignore the stories he'd heard about carnivorous barrow bats inhabiting such places. He had avoided asking Biter if they were real, in case it turned out that they were. When his hauberk snagged on the sculpted foot of a knight's effigy protruding from another plinth, he freed himself with a quick tug and a reminder to concentrate on moving quickly but respectfully. Being a funeral bearer was a great responsibility.

Ahead of him, holding Sir Halfdan's feet, Symon turned and bent forward. Odo followed, and together the bearers settled the fallen knight on his final resting place.

When that was done, Odo stepped back and bowed.

Outside, Runnel twitched. Eleanor drew her from her scabbard, raising the sword in sad salute. A gray light shimmered along the blade, reflections from the cloudy sky.

"Be at peace, knight of Lenburh," said the blind old man. He turned and tapped the way to the village hall, following the sound of the bell. The villagers followed him, grim-faced. They had much to discuss.

"Our lands cannot stand unprotected!" cried Gladwine, whose sheep grazed the southeast meadows. "Without a steward, we are vulnerable to any passing thief or brigand!"

"How will we find a new one?" demanded Leof the woodworker.

"Who will guard us?" went up the cry from several people.

"Not these *children*," scowled Elmer, Addyson and Aaric's father. His sharp eyes took in Eleanor and Odo where they sat to either side of Egda and Hundred at the front of the hall.

"We'd do a better job than a baker," muttered Eleanor, resenting the implication that they wouldn't be good enough. They were knights. They had fought serious enemies and had stared down a real, live dragon — or at least they'd survived an encounter with one, which was more than most people could say, Elmer included.

"I have sent word by pigeon to Winterset," said Symon across the restless crowd's murmuring. "My colleagues in the capital will report to the regent, who will appoint the next steward."

"How long will that take?" asked Swithe the leatherworker, who had wanted to skin the bilewolves before burning but found the hides too foul-smelling for any purpose. "What if more of those terrible creatures come?"

"There will be no more," said Hundred in a clear and steady voice. "I traced the pack's spoor to a hollow where a craft-fire recently burned. This fire was lit to summon the bilewolves and send them against my liege."

This was news to Odo, who struggled to keep the shock from his face. Someone had *deliberately* called the beasts that had killed four of his fellow villagers? As well as Sir Halfdan and Squire Bordan, Lenburh had lost Halthor, an apprentice smith, and Alia, who had moved from Enedham last year to look after her sick aunt.

A flame of sudden rage burned in his chest.

"Can we track the person who lit the fire?" he asked in a pinched voice. "They must be brought to justice."

"They will be long gone from here now," Hundred said with finality. "Our best hope of finding them is to wait until they try again."

"We'll be ready when they do," said Eleanor, patting Runnel's hilt. The swords stayed silent during the meeting, knowing that some in the village were still unnerved by their enchanted nature.

Elmer snorted. Egda's beaked nose swiveled to point directly at him. The baker swallowed whatever further comments about the young knights' competence he might have offered.

"You will be ready," Egda said, "and Lenburh will be safe, for I am leaving at tomorrow's dawn."

A gasp rose up from all assembled. Only Hundred was unsurprised.

"So soon, sire?" asked Reeve Gorbold, who Odo had overheard making plans to profit from Egda's presence by charging villagers in the area a halfpenny to see the former king in his new home.

"Word of trouble in the capital reached me in my self-imposed exile," Egda said. "Winterset is my destination. Besides, I cannot remain here and put innocent lives at risk. Better to continue on my journey north and east and cut the source of our troubles from the kingdom once and for all."

Eleanor felt a stirring of excitement in her gut. After a month of waiting for something to happen, an adventure had come right to her doorstep.

"We must accompany you, sire," she said, leaping to her feet and drawing Runnel in one swift movement. "We will be your honor guard!"

"If you would have us," said Odo, doing the same, but more cautiously. Biter clashed against his sister's steel with a ringing chime over Egda's head. "We do not wish to impose."

A flicker passed across Hundred's face. Was it a smile? If so, was it of gratitude or amusement?

"My liege needs no honor guard," she said. "He has me, and we travel fast and light into unknown danger —"

"That's why you need us," Eleanor insisted. "Because it's unknown."

"Numbers are no substitute for experience, knightling."

Eleanor ground her teeth. Were they always to come unstuck on this point? "But there's only one way to gain experience, and if you won't let us —"

"Your place is in Lenburh," Egda pronounced. "I must

return to Winterset and see what my great-nephew Kendryk has wrought."

Odo frowned over this piece of information, wondering at its import. If the old king was displeased with his heir and tried to take back the throne, could that lead to unrest in the court, perhaps even civil war? Tofte had been peaceful for many generations, all the way back to King Mildred the Marvelous. The thought of villager fighting villager again was a terrible one.

That was reason enough to accompany Egda, to ensure no trouble came to the young Prince Kendryk. After all, Odo and Eleanor ultimately owed their fealty to him, the heir to the throne, not to Egda or even to their home . . .

Before Eleanor, following the same reasoning, could find a diplomatic way to press for their inclusion in the party journeying to the nation's capital, a horn sounded outside the guildhall, then a rapid patter of running feet came near. The doors burst open.

"Strangers!" cried a wide-eyed lad half Odo's age. "Lots and lots and lots of them, on horses!"

"*More* strangers?" gasped Reeve Gorbold. "What are the odds of that?"

"Very small, I hazard to say," said Symon with a thoughtful expression. "Lenburh has never seen such a flood."

A babble of speculation rippled through the gathering, and Egda rapped the end of his staff against the floorboards for silence.

"Reeve Gorbold, perhaps you should invite them in."

"But name no names," warned Hundred. "We are not here."

"Of course, sire, uh, madam, of course." The reeve bowed in confusion and hurried from the hall.

Odo and Eleanor exchanged a glance and followed as fast as their armor allowed, holding their swords at the ready.

"What if it's the people who sent the bilewolves?" Odo whispered at Eleanor's back.

"I don't hear any howling or snarling, do you?" she cast over her shoulder.

"We are a match for any beast!" Biter declared.

"Be wary, little brother," Runnel cautioned. "Someone with the skill to light a craft-fire is a worthy foe. Not to mention the person who commands them."

Eleanor gripped her sword tightly and hurried out into the light, where she came face-to-bridle with a band of travelers on horseback, all sporting the royal seal on their breasts — a blue shield, quartered, with a silver sword, a black anvil, a red flame, and a golden dragon in each segment. All the new arrivals were armed, although none had unsheathed a weapon. At their head rode a tall, thin man wearing an unfamiliar red uniform with silver piping, topped by a wide-brimmed cloth hat, which he raised on seeing the reeve's chain of office, and then again for the two young knights.

"Well met, bereaved citizens of Lenburh," he said, holding the hat now at his chest, revealing a pate of fine white hair, brushed in a spiral descending from the top of his head. "Rest your troubled hearts, for I have come to give you ease."

"And you are?" Reeve Gorbold asked.

"Instrument Sceam," said the man with a brisk bow from his waist.

"Your name is 'Instrument'?" Eleanor repeated in puzzlement.

"Instrument is my title. I have been sent to assume the mantle of responsibility so recently vacated by Sir Halfdan."

"Sent by whom?" bristled the reeve.

"By the regent, of course," said Sceam with another bow.

"So you're to be our steward?" Odo asked.

"Not steward," the man said. "*Instrument*. Of the Crown."

"But we don't know you," said Eleanor.

"That hardly matters, does it?"

Reeve Gorbold straightened with a sniff. "Only people whose families have lived in Lenburh five generations can be stewards. That's the rule."

"The rule has changed. May I come in and explain?"

"You'd better come, I suppose. Your horses will be attended to."

"My thanks, Reeve Gorbold."

"You know my name?"

"And those of your young companions also, Sir Odo and Sir Eleanor. I know everything about you."

"But . . . how? What are you *doing* here?"

Instrument Sceam dropped lightly to the ground and produced a rolled-up parchment from one pocket. It was crumpled and stained brown at one end, as though by blood.

"Why, I received your note."

The message-carrying pigeon informing the capital of Sir Halfdan's death had traveled only as far as Trumness, a town on the mountain road east of Ablerhyll. There it had caught the attention of one of Instrument Sceam's companions, a keen-eyed archer, and been immediately shot down.

"You shot," Reeve Gorbold spluttered, "my pigeon?"

"Of course," Sceam replied.

"But . . . *why*?"

"It was white."

"So?"

"White pigeons are no longer authorized to carry messages to Winterset. Only the speckled variety. This is another of the many changes I have been sent to inform you about."

"What are these changes, exactly?" asked Symon.

"Well . . ." Instrument Sceam placed his hands on his knees and scanned the crowd. He was seated in the place Egda had occupied a moment ago, alone on the raised dais. The former king was wearing a hood that covered the upper half of his face and standing well at the back. Eleanor recognized his nose and the stubborn jut of his jaw, but only because she was looking for it.

Of Hundred there was no sign at all.

"The pigeons, for one." Sceam was happy to have their full attention and showed little sign of letting it go. "All communication with the capital is now limited to official channels, from Instruments such as myself to the Adjustors and the Regulators, who take the messages to the highest level. I have cages of the speckled breed in my baggage for that very purpose. They are not to be used without my express permission."

"Let me see if I understand this correctly," said Symon. "Instruments report to the Adjustors."

"Yes."

"And Adjustors report to the Regulators."

"Yes."

"To whom do Regulators report?"

"To the regent."

"And the regent — Odelyn — reports to Prince Kendryk, the heir?"

"Why, yes, of course. It is only proper that the regent keeps young Prince Kendryk informed for . . . ee . . . educational reasons at the least."

Sceam's smile was wide and seemingly sincere, although there was something in his eyes that made Eleanor's hackles rise. Perhaps it was the familiar way he referred to the regent, the old king's sister, and the dismissive tone he used for her grandson, the young heir who had not yet been crowned.

Or perhaps it was something more immediate.

"Where do knights fit in?" Eleanor asked.

"Ah. As traditional stewards of the estates of Tofte, these honored individuals will of course be found a role in the new system."

"What kind of role?"

"It's not my place to say. Something ceremonial, I imagine, such as standing by doorways in the capital to make them look more regal. You will be told in due course."

Odo felt Biter stirring in his scabbard in response to the word *ceremonial*. No sword wanted to end up on display, doing nothing but growing dull with time and dust. No knight either.

"There must be some kind of mistake," Odo started to say, but was cut off by a frail-seeming but penetrating voice from the back of the room.

"Forgive me, I am an old blind man, and hard of hearing to boot . . . This new system I believe I heard you speak of . . . is it the work of Prince Kendryk himself?"

"Of course," Sceam said, not recognizing his interlocutor. "The regent made the announcement on his behalf three months ago. Implementation throughout the kingdom is well under way, although outlying regions such as this one are naturally behind schedule. We will soon make that up, now that I am here!"

The Instrument clapped his hands in eagerness to get started.

"My collectors will move among you over the coming week," he declared, "collecting this month's tithe."

"But Sir Halfdan paid the Crown just *last* week!" spluttered Reeve Gorbold.

"I'm afraid there's no record of that in the capital," Sceam said. "Also, from this month, tithes will increase by five silver pennies per household."

"What?!" the reeve exclaimed, but he was far from the only person in the room to think it.

"To cover the costs of instituting the new system. Prosperity has its price!"

"This is preposterous —"

"It is *progress*, Reeve Gorbold. Now, I am weary. I will retire to the manor house to rest. No need to show me. I know the way."

With that, he stood and pressed through the dumbfounded crowd, flanked by two of his well-armed aides. Eleanor went to step into his path, unwilling to let the matter of this "new system" go so readily. She hadn't spent her whole life dreaming of being a knight only to end up standing around in a doorway holding a pike!

Before she could take half a step, however, a small but very strong hand gripped her elbow.

"Discretion," whispered Hundred into Eleanor's ear, "is our best stratagem at this time."

Eleanor frowned at the old woman. How would saying nothing be of any use to anyone?

"We will talk around the back," Hundred reassured her, nodding to where Odo was being led off by Symon, with Egda bringing up a close rear.

Under cover of Sceam's departure, the five of them slipped from the guildhall by the tradesperson's door.

THREE

This cannot stand," said Egda.

"*Never has a truer word been spoken!*" exclaimed Biter, lunging out of Odo's scabbard and flashing about the smithy in which they huddled, well out of earshot of Sceam and his cronies. The furnace was cold out of respect for the dead apprentice. "*My siege, let us slay the upstarts while they rest, before their unrighteous hold of the estate is established!*"

Odo expected the former king to scold Biter for being too rash, as Odo himself always did, but he was surprised.

"Yes, Biter, I believe you are half right, at least." Egda leaned on his staff, looking all his years but no less determined. "Slaying should not be necessary, but it is time for direct action."

"Sire," said Hundred, "you must not openly declare yourself."

"That would be unwise," Symon agreed. "If the Crown is truly behind this strange new system —"

"It is not Kendryk," Egda interrupted with surprising venom. "This must be the regent's doing. Odelyn was ever ambitious. I hoped she would be true, but it is clear she is loyal to nothing other than her own desires and ambition.

Kendryk's coronation has been delayed long past his turning sixteen, and treacherous efforts have been made to keep this news from me, and from all at the Temple of Midnight where I formerly made my home. Now I must help Kendryk claim his proper birthright. Odelyn cannot prevail against both of us."

"If it is not too late," observed Hundred. "We have perhaps tarried here too long already."

"You can't leave us with Sceam, that . . ." Eleanor fought for a fittingly cutting phrase. ". . . that slimy cumberwold!"

"We will not," Egda promised her, reaching out to pat her shoulder. "He will be dealt with tonight, once the moon has set."

"Do you have a plan, sire?" asked Runnel, standing point-down at Eleanor's side, her ruby gleaming a soft bloodred. "More detailed than my brother's, I mean."

"I do. We need six able-bodied volunteers. Master Symon, can you enlist them to our cause?"

Eleanor's father nodded. "I could find a dozen without taking as many steps."

"Very good. Light footfalls would be valuable, also."

"Understood, sire."

"Hundred? Settle on a rendezvous point while I address our knights and their swords."

Egda turned to Odo and Eleanor as Symon and Hundred conversed in hushed voices.

"Sir Odo, Sir Eleanor: Tonight, we fight for Lenburh, as you have fought bravely once already. I have no compunction concerning your courage when called upon to act in the teeth of the moment, but with forethought . . . and in consideration of your tender age . . . I wonder if you might prefer to watch this battle from the gallery."

"Not fight with you?" Eleanor couldn't believe what she was hearing. "Don't be mad — I mean . . . sorry, sire . . . but we're knights, not shirkers!"

"Our place is by your side," Odo agreed with a vigorous nod.

"It is kind of you to worry, sire," said Runnel. "Although they may be young, Odo and Eleanor have drawn blood against beasts with two legs as well as four."

"The dragon Quenwulf herself decreed them knights in truth," agreed Biter, sweeping back into Odo's hand and lifting his arm in a salute. "We are your eager servants!"

Egda nodded, the corners of his lips turning up in a smile. "It seems I have little choice in the matter. Against noble hearts, one rarely does. You will follow Hundred's lead as we advance together on the manor house. Together, we will do what must be done — and quickly, ere Instrument Sceam and his lackeys recover from their long journey. Those who break the rules of chivalry do not deserve chivalry in return."

He paused, then added, "We must refrain from killing anyone, if we can. They are in some sense servants of the Crown, and though greedy varlets, they do not deserve to die."

At sun's fall, Eleanor's father and the others gathered behind a hedge near the Dry Well. Hundred kept watch as Symon made introductions. He had brought along the six largest men and women in Lenburh, Odo's mother and the baker among them, all with their staves. Odo wondered at Elmer being there, but decided that against a common enemy, all were united. Besides, the baker was as strong as Odo from carrying sacks of flour.

"Sir Odo, Sir Eleanor, Hundred, and myself will lead the assault," Egda explained. "We will enter from the rear, subduing and restraining any guards we find. You have your lengths of rope, Eleanor, Odo? Good. Symon, you and your stout allies will take positions in the grounds to ensure all exits are sealed from within and without. Reinforcements must be stalled, and none must escape to spread the word of what happens here. Remember, knock them down, but refrain from killing if you can."

"Understood, sire," said Symon.

"Four against seven?" said Elmer. He had the good grace not to add, "one of them blind and two of them children?" for which Eleanor gave him credit. "What if you run into trouble?"

"Then your aid will be invaluable. Listen for Hundred's horn. If you hear it, come running."

"Aye, sire."

Symon daubed his face black with charcoal to hide better in the darkness, and in a few moments he had attended to the others.

Hundred returned.

"All clear," she whispered, her breath little more than a breeze in the night.

"Very well," said Egda. "We begin."

Biter and Runnel slipped silently from their sheaths and joined their knights in readiness. As Symon and his six strong-arms slid off into the darkness, Hundred took the lead, moving in a rapid crouch towards the estate. Odo followed, watching his tread carefully to avoid dry twigs. Eleanor came after him, nearly as quiet as Hundred, and behind her, last of all, Egda, moving with confident stealth, his hood tugged low over his face, well used to the darkness that impeded the others.

An owl called "Who!" as the four humans passed beneath her branch. Swiveling her head from side to side in case their footfalls disturbed any cowering mice, she suddenly froze, then launched with deadly speed into the air. An instant later, there came a tiny, short-lived squeak, and she flew to her favorite perch to eat her first snack of the evening.

There was a guard posted to the rear of the manor house, a long-limbed woman who had nodded off with her chin propped up on the cross-bar of her boar spear. Eleanor looked around for Hundred, but she had disappeared. Seconds later she darted out of the trees and brought the guard down with one hand across her mouth and a forearm tight against her throat.

The guard struggled for a minute, then fell unconscious. Odo and Eleanor bound her limbs while Egda tied a gag across her mouth. Hundred took the boar spear and the guard's dagger away and hid them in the bushes.

"Gag, bind, remove weapons," she whispered.

Odo and Eleanor nodded. Hundred made it look easy,

but both knew it wouldn't be. Odo felt Biter shift in his hand, and held the sword tighter. Biter might well need to be restrained from delivering killing blows.

As soundless as a shadow, Hundred opened the door and eased inside.

Eleanor went next, wishing her mail didn't make so much noise. Odo could hear nothing over the sound of snoring that issued from the interior of the manor. The main hall, it quickly became clear, had been taken over by Sceam's entourage. Six sleeping figures sprawled on their bedrolls, lit by flickering candles and the remains of a fire. Sceam was the closest to the warmth, curled into a ball.

Odo tallied up the numbers and concluded that there must be another guard at the front door.

Hundred held a finger to her lips and tiptoed among the sleeping figures, removing weapons from their owners with the dexterity of a pickpocket. The collection of daggers and swords she quickly accumulated went behind a tapestry that lapped down to the flagstones behind the front door.

Then she pointed Odo at one guard, Eleanor at another, and made a clicking noise with her tongue next to a third, which Egda followed to position himself close to that sleeper. They all sheathed their weapons and readied lengths of rope.

With everyone in position, Hundred held up three fingers, closed one, then another, and then, with the last, suddenly seized the sleeper in front of her as the others did the same to theirs, swiftly trussing them up like livestock, wrists tied to ankles.

This was done so quickly that by the time their confused shouts had woken the last two guards, Odo and Hundred had already finished their first lot and were onto them. One guard sprang up with a dagger, but Hundred gripped his wrist and twisted his arm until he shrieked and fell to his knees, dropping the weapon. Odo simply clapped the one who came at him on the shoulder blade, sending him straight back down again. Both were tied up in a moment, as Eleanor and Egda closed in on Sceam, who had gotten wrapped up in his cloak and was struggling to free himself.

Eleanor bent down and pulled the cloak away. Sceam's head popped out, his expression outraged.

"How dare you! Guards! Guards!"

The front door burst in, admitting the single remaining guard. But Odo and Hundred were ready. Hundred tripped the guard and Odo fell on him, one knee pinning him to the ground as Hundred removed his sword and they both tied him up.

"You can't do this!" screeched Sceam. "I am an Instrument of the Crown!"

Hundred drew a shining leaf-shaped blade and held it up in front of the Instrument, moving the knife slowly back and forth.

"Who . . . who are you?" asked Sceam nervously, his eyes following the glint of the blade. "What do you want?"

"Remind him who you are, Sir Odo, Sir Eleanor," Egda said.

"We're the knights of Lenburh," said Eleanor, drawing herself up to her full height. Possibly this was less impressive than she intended, as she was shorter than Sceam.

"And we don't take kindly to being told we're no longer needed," added Odo.

"D-did I say that?" Sceam said, nearly babbling. "I'm s-sorry I gave you that impression —"

"Ceremonial, you said." Biter leaped out of his scabbard, evading Odo's attempt to grab him. The sword swung in a lethal arc until his tip pointed directly at the Instrument's fast-beating heart. "The word leaves little room for ambiguity."

Sceam's eyes widened at the sword's short speech, but he seemed less afraid of the sword than he was of Hundred. His sharp eyes had spotted that his guards were tied up, rather than lying dead. Clearly his enemies were afraid of doing any real damage to persons of his importance.

"You don't know what you're dealing with," he spat. "The times are changing, and you can't fight it — not with steel or spells or other old-fashioned notions. This is the age of opportunity, where anyone can rise regardless of birth or wealth. Stand in our way and you will be trampled."

"Is that what Regent Odelyn tells you?" Egda asked. "Her age of opportunity applies only to herself. And she does not have the right to do what she has done."

"Bah!" Sceam tried to sit up straighter, but quailed back as Biter shivered in front of him. "The regent has done only what *must* be done! Prince Kendryk is weak. He is not fit to rule. His hours are spent in the palace, idly doodling. The boy has lost his mind! The regent does not want power for herself, but to take it away from a mad-man for the good of the people —"

"Take it away?" Egda interrupted. "Do you mean Odelyn intends to crown herself? To be king and not just regent?"

"The prince is unfit to rule," said Sceam sullenly. "The king — *Regent* Odelyn — is doing only what is necessary. Now, you yokels have had your fun. Regulator Ardrahei has twenty . . . no, *fifty* guards with him, and if he doesn't receive a pigeon from me after dawn, he'll come looking, and then you'll all be locked up in irons! If you disperse now, I will be merciful. Go!"

No one moved.

"You think you've won," snarled Sceam. "You are wrong. Regulator Ardrahei and the regent will hear of what has happened here —"

"That I doubt very much," said Egda. "And even if they do, they will simply know what happens to people who ignore the ancient customs."

"Regulator Ardrahei will come, with his *eighty guards* —"

"And we will fight them. The four of us, who dealt so easily with the eight of you." Egda gestured with one hand, encompassing the roped-up fighters. "Have no fear on our account. Hundred? It is time."

The woman nodded and drew out a small, gold-banded horn and sounded it, its harsh call echoing through the hall and beyond.

A minute later, Symon and the other six burst into the manor through the front and back.

"What is this?" Elmer asked, looking about him in confusion at the disarmed men and women tied up on the floor. "Where's the fight?"

"Temporarily delayed," Hundred told him.

"Take this man to the lockup," Egda instructed the baker. "He's to be treated well but denied access to writing materials and pigeons, be they speckled or otherwise. Lock the others in with him. Keep them there until you receive word from Winterset. Hundred, give them a gold noble for the prisoner's upkeep."

"No need on that score," Elmer said, taking a protesting Sceam about the collar and lifting him with strong arms. "I think I have some moldy loaves left from last week, perhaps a pot of rancid butter or two . . ."

"Does this mean you're our new steward, sire?" asked Odo's mother, with a surprisingly humble tug at her forelock.

Egda inclined his head in regret. "You do me a great honor . . . but I think Master Symon would fit the role better than I."

"Me, sire?" Symon looked momentarily startled, then bowed deeply. "Until the prince is crowned king and appoints a proper replacement for Sir Halfdan, I will serve . . . if the others will have me."

"Aye," said Elmer. "You'll do. You're fair, even if you do think too much."

That was as close to a compliment as the baker ever came, and Eleanor was amazed to hear it. Symon bowed again, and Elmer dragged Sceam out of the manor and down the hill, shaking him all the way. Odo's mother and the rest retied the Instrument's guards into a hobbled line and quickly followed, encouraging the crestfallen Instrument's companions with taps from their staves.

When they were gone, Symon turned to Egda with a wry smile.

"You never had any intention of us fighting, did you, sire?"

The former king swept back his hood and straightened it. "No. I merely wished to see if people would follow you. And they did. Therefore, you would make a good steward. I would appoint you permanently were it my place to."

Eleanor beamed in pride. Her father, acting steward of Lenburh!

"What next?" asked Odo. "First the bilewolves, and then this lot —"

"They are not necessarily connected," said Hundred.

"Perhaps," said Egda. "Although I suspect both actions do arise from the same source."

Hundred nodded thoughtfully, then turned back to the others. "My liege and I passed through Lenburh only because it's on the river road, so we might have missed Sceam entirely if the master of the bilewolves had chosen a different moment to make their move. A mixture of fortunes for both of us."

"I hope that rescuing you from one problem makes up for bringing another to your door," said Egda.

"Think nothing of it," said Symon. "If we can be of assistance, you have but to ask."

"I beg only for provisions," said the former king. "My intention remains to leave at dawn."

Dawn! Eleanor sensed an opportunity slipping through her fingers. She couldn't bear the thought of just wishing for adventure, as she had been only yesterday, instead of having one.

"You must let us come with you!" exclaimed Eleanor. "Especially now you know it's probably the regent who sent the bilewolves. You need us to protect you!"

"Eleanor is right," said Odo heavily. He really didn't want to leave Lenburh again, not so soon. He could tell from Eleanor's shining eyes she was looking forward to adventure, where he only felt the weight of responsibility. But like stacking sacks of flour at the mill, this was an essential task that wouldn't just happen, and more hands made lighter and safer work. "We can't let you go on your own."

"With two knights," said Symon, "and two enchanted swords, you would better your odds against the prince's adversaries."

"What about your daughter's safety?" Egda asked him.

"By helping you restore peace to the kingdom, she will ensure that she has a home to return to. The same goes for Odo and his parents too."

"You are wise, Steward Symon," said Egda, with a gracious nod at the two young knights. "Now that I know you two follow orders as bravely as you rush into battle, I would be grateful to you both if you will join me on this quest as cadets in the royal — no, I suppose I must call it the former king's guard."

Eleanor gaped in surprise, momentarily lost for words. She had expected an argument, but it turned out the old man had been one step ahead of everyone again . . .

"Sire, it will be an honor," said Odo with a quick bow to cover his feelings of apprehension. He wasn't frightened of any adversaries he might meet along the way, but being thrust into the world of Winterset and the court was daunting. Sir Halfdan's original promise to take them there had dragged on until it seemed likely never to happen. Now it was about to become a reality, and he didn't feel ready to leave his home.

"On foot, it will take a month or more to reach the capital," said Symon. "You should take the horses — two each, plus two for baggage. Sceam won't be needing them."

"And you will send the speckled pigeons to Winterset," said Hundred, "with false reports that Sceam is securely installed?"

"Of course. That will gain you some time." Symon took Eleanor in a quick embrace and nodded at Odo over her shoulder. "Travel safely and fight well. Remember what Quenwulf told you."

"Knights be true," she said, nodding.

"And swords?"

Biter flew out of Odo's hand. "Do not grow rusty!"

"In mind or steel!" Runnel finished in more measured tones.

Dragon, dragon, heed our call . . .

From within the uppermost spire of Winterset Castle came the sound of a young man humming.

Come to aid us, one and all . . .

"I know that tune," said the young man's grandmother. "Don't think I don't know what you're singing in here."

The young man paused at his work, concentration broken. A long shadow reached across the wall in front of him, a silhouette anyone in Tofte would recognize, thanks to its nose. Proud and angular, it had graced kings of Tofte for three hundred years. She had it, her brother had had it, and the young man had it too.

He looked down at his crimson-spattered hands and attempted to gather his thoughts. If he could just complete the next section of his mural by nightfall, his mind would feel so much more at ease.

Dragon, dragon, heed our call . . .

His beaky-nosed grandmother had other ideas.

"I've just come from the Privy Council," she said, her voice smug. "They've voted unanimously to put off the coronation indefinitely."

She paused, her mouth curving back into a smile, before continuing.

"*Your* coronation, I mean. However, the *next* coronation has been brought forward and will take place in three days. Mine, that is. Can't leave the kingdom without a proper ruler any longer. I will be king. How does that make you feel?"

Prince Kendryk hung his head. Red was plastered all down the front of what had once been an extremely fine robe featuring a tiny, recurring motif of the royal seal. Now it was stiff and, frankly, not terribly comfortable. He kept it on, though. Clothes were much harder to do without than sandals. His last pair had worn out and he had given up asking for them to be replaced. His grandmother enjoyed enforcing such petty deprivations.

"Leave me alone, Grandmother," he said. "I'm busy."

"Ah, it speaks. I was beginning to wonder if you'd forgotten how."

"I have nothing to say to you."

"But you'll sing that nonsense children's song in the hope that the old fool will come rescue you — the one who left a baby heir behind in swaddling clothes because he lost his nerve? I know that's what you're doing: 'Old Dragon' nonsense. I think he was always more of a lizard, my oh-so-great brother Egda. I suppose he couldn't bear the thought of people calling him 'Old *Blind* Dragon' . . . old *fool*, more like —"

Prince Kendryk closed his eyes and concentrated to block out her rant. The song was his lifeline, a shining thread leading to a future where he was no longer badgered by the woman who had driven his mother to an early grave and would be only too happy to see him in his.

Dragon, dragon, heed our call . . .

"Pah," she exclaimed. "You're as mad as they say you are if you think a song will bring that sightless dullard here. And if it did, what could he do? He's blind and useless. Probably dead now, for all we know. A sudden attack of bilewolves, perhaps . . ."

She smiled again, waiting briefly for a response that never came, then walked away with a snap of her fingers for her shadow and chief servant, a black-haired man who did the regent's every bidding with a smile that was too wide for any sane person's liking. A massive sword hung at his waist, brutal and cruel, with an empty setting where a gem had once been fastened.

"Let us leave this half-wit to his idle pastimes, Lord Deor. We have important affairs of state to attend to."

"Yes, Your Highness."

"Grandmother?"

She stopped and turned, her heels squeaking on stone.

"Yes, Kendryk? You've changed your mind? You will officially abdicate and resign any right to the throne? It isn't necessary, of course, but it would be . . . convenient."

The young prince tilted his head back and pointed into the uppermost gloom of the spire.

"There are bats up there," he said. "I hear them squeaking."

"What of it?"

"They're trapped. I would like the porters to open a shutter or two so they can escape."

"And why should I do that?"

"Maybe I will sign the paper. If the bats are freed."

"Bats and daubing paint! I should put you in a cage and hang it from the city gates so everyone can see your idiocy!"

Muttering irritably, the regent stomped off, slamming the door behind her.

Prince Kendryk lowered his gaze to the wall in front of him. The mural was incomplete, but he was free to resume now. He had made great progress in recent months. The end was at last in sight. Perhaps a week and it would be done, if he wasn't interrupted again.

Stooping to place both hands in the bucket of red paint, he began once more to daub thick lines on the ancient, black stone of Winterset, humming all the while.

Dragon, dragon, heed our call.

Come to aid us, one and all.

Half an hour later, as the city bells tolled seven, he paused briefly, hearing the slow grind of the shutters opening overhead. The bats were being set free.

That meant his grandmother did need him to sign the abdication papers, no matter what she said.

But he wouldn't, Kendryk told himself. He wouldn't do anything she wanted. He turned back to his painting.

From a cruel and dreadful fate,

Save us now, ere it's too late.

Both Odo and Eleanor had ridden horses on occasion, usually the farmer Gladwine's old nag Pudding, who had a good nature provided there were plenty of apples on offer.

Never in their lives had they ridden like this, on fine riding horses, leading fresh remounts.

Both were weary, having slept restlessly, albeit for very different reasons. Odo had tossed and turned, imagining the many obstacles that might stand between Lenburh and Winterset, until eventually his two nearest older brothers begged him to get out of bed and leave them to their rest. As a result, at dawn he had not just been packed and ready, but the earliest to arrive at the rendezvous point by the stump of Lightning Tree, and thus gained the first choice of mount.

Eleanor's restless night had come from imagining the very same things as Odo, only to her they were not obstacles but opportunities. She imagined herself following in her mother's footsteps, battling monsters, defeating villains, and gathering more fame and glory with every mile. The simple act of seating herself a-horse made her feel very grand, which was a good start.

At Hundred's cry of "Let us hie hence!" they set out from Lenburh along the river road, heading north, alternating between a steady canter and a walk. None of them was wearing armor; this, plus sufficient supplies for one week, was carried by the two baggage horses. When the steeds they rode grew tired, they would swap to those that ran unburdened alongside them. That way they would make maximum progress without dangerously exhausting any of the animals.

The road was good and the weather fair. In the slower stretches, Egda asked them about Quenwulf, and they told him the story with only occasional theatrical interruption from Biter. With astonishing speed, they came to the turnoff to Ablerhyll Road, and followed it northwest, into territory Eleanor and Odo hadn't visited before. Near a small hamlet called Gistern, they stopped at a swift-flowing brook to stretch their legs and water the horses. Odo's thighs ached; he wasn't used to riding and tended to grip too hard with his legs. Eleanor had an easier time of it, being both more practiced and lighter. Hundred gave her the task of changing the saddles and checking the packs containing their armor and supplies. Nothing appeared to be loose, but it still had to be done.

As Odo stretched his aching legs, he studied Egda. The old man had a new, tense set to his jaw, and he stood alone, facing silently back the way they had come. He looked regretful, almost angry.

"Is Egda all right?" Odo whispered to Hundred. "Does he think we've left something behind?"

"Only ghosts," she said, not looking at him.

Odo glanced at Eleanor, but she hadn't heard. Then he looked back at Hundred. Did she mean actual ghosts? he wondered. Surely not . . .

Soon they were up and riding again, and so it continued until dusk, when they halted for the night. This time both young knights were given chores to perform as they made camp in a tidy copse bordered by blackberry bushes. They brushed down the horses and gave them feed, then lit a fire, caught two rabbits, dug a necessary trench, and made dinner.

The meal left them feeling heavy and sleepy, but there were more tasks to perform. Bedrolls had to be laid out, dirty clothes aired and checked for fleas and other unwanted passengers. Neither Odo nor Eleanor had gone to such lengths on their one other epic journey; former kings clearly required better treatment.

"Who cares about the best way to lay out a blanket?" Eleanor muttered under her breath. "We're knights, not inn servants. We should be practicing swordplay!"

"The best knights are humble and consider no skill beneath them," Runnel chastised her. "For instance, Sir Hollis, my first knight, was an excellent carpenter. Sir Faline could cook to make a gourmand weep, and Sir Treddian's stitches were ever tiny and neat —"

"You're not helping, Runnel," Eleanor complained.

Biter made a rasping noise that Odo had learned to equate with clearing his throat. "I hate to disagree with my more experienced sister —"

"Really?" said Runnel. "That's never stopped you."

"But I do feel that Sir Eleanor raises an excellent point. Our knights have much yet to learn. How are we to teach them when every waking moment is taken up with chores?"

"Being a knight isn't all about fighting," Odo said. In fact, in his opinion, the less fighting, the better.

"No, but we have to be ready to fight when we need to," Eleanor grumbled. "Sometimes I really think we got the wrong swords . . ."

When it was finally time to settle in for the night, they found Egda in his bedroll with Hundred keeping watch nearby, patiently sharpening one of the many blades she kept in her pockets.

"Is the fire high enough, sire?" she asked.

Only it wasn't her voice. She sounded like a man, deep and husky.

"Aye, Beremus. It is well stoked and raging."

Eleanor and Odo hesitated on the edge of the campsite, wondering what was going on. The fire was banked, only coals being kept for the morning.

"Even the coldest night will pass with a tune to warm your heart."

That was Hundred again, in yet another voice, this time a woman's, but younger than her own and more musical.

Egda sighed. "Peg, your lute would comfort a dead man. Give us a round of 'Drunk Eyes Fair See What Fair Not Be,' would you? It'll put Beremus in the mood for a laugh, and by the stars, he needs one."

Hundred hummed a few bars of the bawdy song, but her voice was rough and there was definitely no lute to accompany her.

Egda sighed again, and this time raised his cooling tea in a mournful salute. "To all the friends we've farewelled down the years," he said.

"To all the friends," Hundred echoed. "Where have those knightlings gotten to?"

Eleanor cleared her throat and stepped into view. "Yes, well," she said, sensing that they had interrupted something private and pretending that she and Odo were too deep in conversation to have noticed, "I maintain that Clover Gorbold is the only girl in Lenburh fit to marry a knight. She may be three years older than you and interested only in geegaws, but she is the reeve's daughter. I'm sure her collection of polished stones would grow on you in time."

Catching on, Odo joined in. "What about you? The acting steward's daughter *and* a knight? You'll have to leave town to find an available prince — or maybe a number of them will duel for you on the green."

"They'd be fools, then. As if I would be impressed by anyone who wasn't dueling with *me*."

Eleanor folded herself on top of her bedroll, shifting her weight onto one hip to spare her aching backside. Perched on a flat stone in front of her, she found a steaming mug that smelled like heaven after a long day in the saddle. A second sat in front of Odo, and he sipped gratefully from it.

"You are young to think of marriage," said Egda.

Neither Odo nor Eleanor saw the twinkle returning to his eye.

"We're not!" they both protested.

"Just joking about it," said Odo.

"Not much else to joke about in the village," said Eleanor.

"Perhaps it's as well to begin to think about it, even so," mused Egda. "As knights, you will be attractive partners to many. One purpose of the court is to make matches between far-flung families, and many young folk — not quite so young as you two — come to the court to seek suitable marriages. If we survive, I expect you will both be sought after at the many dances and balls and flirtations and whatnot."

Eleanor and Odo exchanged horrified glances.

Hundred surprised Odo and Eleanor with a smirk. "More for you both to learn! There are at least twenty different dances, not to mention the language of flowers — you know what the different colored roses mean, don't you?"

Odo was far too aware of where they were headed, if all went well and they weren't captured by the regent's Instruments, Regulators, and Adjustors en route. To the royal court — and not just the court, but the castle of Winterset and its surrounds, a city of many thousands.

"I can't imagine it," he said, his voice suddenly weak and small. "So many people in one place. So many strangers."

"Have no fear, Sir Odo," said Biter, nudging the sharpening stone and oil closer to him. "I will take care of you as you take care of me."

"Oh, I'm not worried about that," Odo said, taking the hint and beginning to clean his sword. "It's just . . . everyone will be *looking* at us."

"You won't be the object of their attention," said Egda. "The court will be watching the people *around* you, to see whose favor you have won. If you are alone, you will be perceived vulnerable. If you attract a crowd, they will think you strong."

"Crowds are like dragons," Hundred said with a sniff. "Half as smart as they think they are, and not nearly as powerful. Pay them no heed."

"Do you miss the court?" asked Eleanor, stifling a yawn.

"Never," said the old woman, but Egda was silent. He seemed to have gone to sleep, or was maintaining a determined pretense.

"If you're tired, Biter and Runnel can keep watch," Odo said to Hundred, thinking that she must be as exhausted as he and Eleanor were, probably more so, given her age.

She shook her head. "They're welcome to stay up and keep me company if they like, but I'll not trust the life of my liege to ancient swords, particularly when one of them can't remember how he ended up at the bottom of a river, and the other once thought she was cursed. No offense, either of you. You're good in battle, but I cannot bring myself to trust you."

With that she closed one eye and went very still.

Odo waited a good minute before concluding that Hundred was literally half asleep. That way she could keep watch all night and still get some rest, albeit half that of someone sleeping normally.

"What's the river got to do with anything?" muttered Biter, quivering gently under Odo's oiling rag.

"She's saying you're unreliable, little brother," said Runnel. "Or are you being rhetorical?"

"Ancient, she said!"

"Be glad she didn't mention that nick you've got as well. You don't remember how you got that either."

"It is no impediment to my performance!"

"Careful, Biter," said Odo, pulling his hands away. "If you get any more worked up, you'll take my fingers off!"

"I am sorry, Sir Odo. She does my nerves no service by being so provocative!"

"Who, me or Hundred?" asked Runnel.

"Both!"

"All right, that's it," said Odo, packing up the oil and rag. "You two can keep arguing if you want, but I'm going to sleep."

"Me too," said Eleanor, surrendering to another yawn. She tugged open her bedroll and slipped inside, feeling disappointed that their first night on the road wasn't filled with stories about the old king's adventures. She had been looking forward to that. Maybe tomorrow morning, when Egda was rested. This was her chance to learn about what her future life would really hold.

Biter and Runnel took positions on opposite sides of the campsite, dividing their time equally between watching the night, watching Hundred, and watching each other.

To Eleanor's continued disappointment, the second day began with more chores, and then they were riding hard for Ablerhyll, changing horses every hour or two. It was too tiring for Egda to talk, or so Hundred maintained. The terrain grew hillier and the road snaked left to right and up and down, crossing rivers and streams on narrow bridges and passing through woods draped with vines and cobwebs. The landscape was dry but heavily farmed, with crops, cattle, and cottages in evidence everywhere they looked. There were few hamlets or villages, however. All roads led to Ablerhyll, it seemed.

The sun was high as they neared the large town, smelling smoke and unwashed humanity in equal measure. Eleanor gazed ahead with something very much like awe. This was the biggest town she had ever seen in her entire life! A dozen spires were visible over the fortified walls, and the smoke from hundreds of chimneys rose up as one and drifted off in a gray fog. It made Lenburh look like a hamlet in comparison.

One of the spires had an odd addition attached near its top, a flimsy-looking cross made of fabric stretched over a wooden frame. It turned slowly in the breeze like the blades of a windmill, but horizontally, more like a water wheel put on its side and stuck on top of the tower. Odo, well versed in how both wind- and water-driven mills worked, wondered what it could possibly be.

This curiosity was not his only emotion. He felt nervous, almost as if they were going into battle, even though they were just planning to pass through the town and continue on the other side. They weren't stopping even for supplies, since Lenburh had provisioned them well, and the lighter they traveled, the better. They would have gone around the town entirely, except it was surrounded by market gardens, irrigation ditches, and walled orchards with no easy way through, so the road through the town was by far the quickest way to proceed.

"Remember," said Egda, lifting his cloak to his chin and tugging his hood forward again, "do not use our real names. I am your grandfather Engelbert, and this is your great-aunt Hilda. You are Otto and Ethel, and we are taking you to be apprenticed in Winterset — Otto with the miller, Ethel with the herbalist."

"Say it back to us," Hundred requested.

They did as they were told, feeling more vulnerable without their real names than they had without their armor, which was still stowed on the baggage horses. Biter and Runnel lay concealed under the saddle blankets of their horses, out of reach but ready to fly forth at the slightest provocation.

It annoyed Eleanor to be hiding the fact that they were knights after so long dreaming of becoming one, although she could see the sense in it.

"Remember," Hundred went on, "there is likely to be an Instrument here, since Ablerhyll is closer to the capital. If we encounter one, act humble and cooperate. Our aim is to pass through unnoticed."

The town gates were open, but there were guards watching all who passed through them. Eleanor felt their hard, suspicious gaze sweep over her and her companions as they approached.

"Do you think they'll recognize us?" she whispered to Runnel.

"Unlikely," said the sword, her voice slightly muffled by the saddle blanket. "Even if they've been alerted about the king, they'll be looking for an older couple on foot, not what looks like a family group on horseback."

"Oh, I hadn't thought of that." Still, she sat ready in her saddle as the guards approached, pikes held at an angle so they crossed, blocking the way.

Egda started telling the guards the story about heading for Winterset to establish his grandchildren in their proper trades, but he told it in a voice that was much lighter and higher-pitched than his own, and included so many unnecessary details — the weather they'd supposedly left, the meals they'd eaten on the way, what people had told them about the road ahead — that the guards soon became restless.

"Cease this blathering, Engelbert," said Hundred in a crone's harsh snap. "Give these good men the toll and we'll be on our way."

Making a show of unhappiness, Egda reached into his saddlebag for a purse. Then, with great reluctance, he proffered each guard a silver penny. They snatched the coins and waved the party on.

"Never fails," said Hundred once the guards were out of earshot. "One good thing about getting old is that nobody takes you seriously anymore."

"Same with being young," Eleanor said.

"True enough." The old warrior turned in her saddle to look at Eleanor and, to Eleanor's utter surprise, winked.

Keeping a close eye on the town's inhabitants, they proceeded along Ablerhyll's crowded main thoroughfare,

Hundred in the lead and Odo bringing up the rear. He kept his horses on a tight rein, wary of slippery mud and loud noises that might see him unseated. The horses were calmer than he was, well used to people and their activities. His anxious gaze soaked up tradespeople hard at work, children playing, stray dogs running between them, and rats eking what living they could from the scraps. There were tiny flies in abundance, and over all a fug that reminded him of his crowded home after a long winter. Through a constant rabble of voices, he could make out what sounded like dozens of cracked bells ringing in the distance.

They passed a market, and the smell of mutton pies made Eleanor's mouth water. She yearned to stop and try one, but there was no room in their mission for dallying. Maybe later, she told herself. When they had defeated the regent, there would be time to eat all the pies she wanted . . .

"Something is not quite right," warned Egda.

Odo nodded. He felt it too. Ever since entering the town, his hackles had been raised, like someone was watching him behind his back. He turned his head both ways, but couldn't see anyone acting out of the ordinary. No one was looking at them at all, as far as he could tell.

"You are perilously exposed," said Biter, the tip of his pommel poking out into view. "I do not like it. An assassin could easily reach your position with a blade thrown from an open window, or from a nearby rooftop with an arrow, or even a dart tipped with aetrenbite poison —"

"Be quiet, little brother," said Runnel. "You will give us away."

Biter subsided, grumbling.

Eleanor looked around her, eyes and ears alert.

"Birds," she said. "I can't hear any."

"Ah, yes," said Egda. "There should be pigeons, sparrows, all the winged scavengers. But the sky is silent."

"Otto and Hilda, look up at the tops of those spires, but carefully, so you won't be noticed," Hundred instructed.

Odo scratched his head and glanced up under cover of his hand.

Perched on the very top of the nearest spire was the largest raven he had ever seen, head crouched low into its feathery blue-black shoulders.

Its gleaming eyes turned to follow them.

Odo glanced to another spire, and another. Each had its raven, and each raven was watching them with a soundless, chilling intensity.

A slight movement caught his eye. There was another raven, much closer, perched atop an eel-seller's stall. It met Odo's gaze, and he saw with a shudder that its eyes were not the normal black of a raven's, but a smoky gray.

Eleanor saw it too.

"The person who sent the bilewolves . . ."

"Yes," said Hundred. "Somewhere, a craft-fire is burning."

"How do they know we're here?"

"They may not. They may simply be watching every traveler on this road."

"So what do we do about them?" asked Eleanor. "Go inside where they can't see us?"

"No," said Egda. "We must not be trapped here. The

best way to avoid an ambush is to move fast, before the jaws can close."

Eleanor wished he had chosen a different metaphor. The poisonous ferocity of the bilewolves was still fresh in her mind.

"We just keep going?" she asked. "And hope nothing gives us away?"

"Precisely," said Hundred. "The road is open ahead. Let's trot. That should not be too suspicious. Simply travelers anxious to make the most of their time."

Eleanor nudged her mount with her knees, and the horse obligingly broke into a trot. Eleanor grimaced as she lifted herself off the saddle in time with the rhythm. The clip-clop of the horse's hooves made a martial drumbeat on the cobbles. Odo fought the urge to look at the birds and concentrated instead on making himself as inconspicuous as possible. He tried whistling nonchalantly, but that only made the lack of birdsong even more obvious. Everyone seemed to be looking at them now, through barred windows or over half-empty barrels, around companions or across tables strewn with wares. With every minute, Odo felt the tension in the small of his back grow.

Finally, when he felt he could take no more, he caught a glimpse of the gate on the far side of the city through a gap between two tall houses whose upper balconies overhung the road. It was so close, just around one more corner and then straight. He felt a surge of relief.

Hundred saw the gate too, but also something else. She raised her hand and everyone reined their mounts back to a walk. They clustered together as they slowly continued.

"The gate is closed," she said quietly. "It shouldn't be closed during the day."

"Show no alarm," said Egda. "When we turn the corner, we'll come to a stop. Odo, act as if your horse has taken a stone in its shoe, while Hundred looks to see what is going on at the gate."

"What if it's closed to keep us in?" asked Eleanor.

"They have no reason to suspect —" began Hundred. But she was suddenly interrupted by a loud voice from behind them.

"Sir Odo! Sir Eleanor! Stop!"

SIX

Eleanor's right hand lunged down the flank of her horse. Runnel was already moving. Barely had the sharkskin grip touched the palm of her hand than she was wheeling around, sword upraised and ready, Odo matching her speed precisely. Runnel and Biter caught the light brilliantly, sweeping forward and down to point at the throat of a man running full tilt towards them.

The man gulped and skidded to a halt just out of reach of the deadly steel. He was old and muscular, with wild, white hair sticking out in odd tufts from under an acorn hat. He stopped so suddenly his hat tipped off and landed in the dirt at his feet. He went to pick it up, then froze as Biter twitched warningly.

"It's me!" the man cried. "Old Ryce. Surprise!"

Odo squinted. It was true. The last time he had seen the ancient machinist — who had been held captive by the false knight Sir Saskia and made to fake a dragon's fire — Old Ryce had been a filthy, ragged figure hurrying up the river road for places unknown. Now he was clean, dressed in a smock covered in pockets, and wearing a new hat. Which was getting muddy on the road.

"Oh, sorry," said Odo, withdrawing Biter. "I didn't recognize you."

"What are you doing here?" asked Eleanor.

"Oh, you know Old Ryce. Working, building — no dragons this time. Never again!"

"You are certain you know this man?" asked Hundred, two jagged throwing knives held at the ready. "He has the look of someone who has experienced evil."

"We definitely know him — and yes, he has," said Eleanor, face pink at the thought of how close she had come to skewering their old friend. "We rescued him from a false knight and he helped us survive a terrible flood."

"Old Ryce is very glad he did too," stammered the old man. "That's my name, and good friends we all are. Hello, Sir Eleanor and Sir Odo! I saw you but you were moving so quickly I almost missed you, Your Honors. But I didn't, did I?"

"Indeed, you did not," said Egda. "However, perhaps now is not the best time for a reunion."

With a furious squawking and flapping of wings, a dozen black shapes converged on them from all sides, claws and beaks reaching for their eyes. Odo ducked and covered his head with one arm. Eleanor lunged her horse forward, out of the cloud of birds. Egda spun his staff overhead, knocking a raven to the ground. Hundred produced a whip and cracked it twice. Three birds fell dead, instantly slain.

That left eight, climbing up to regroup before they dived again.

"We are too exposed here," Hundred said. "More will come!"

None of the birds had attacked Old Ryce, who stood stock-still with his mouth open, dumbfounded. At Hundred's words, he woke from his shock.

"This way! Old Ryce knows where the birds won't go."

He headed off down a narrow side alley at a surprising clip, all elbows and smock flapping around his knees. The others dismounted swiftly, leading their horses. Odo was the first to follow, almost dragging his horse along. She was a headstrong bay with the name "Wiggy" branded into her halter. Where she went, the others would come too — and they did, down the narrow, washing-draped lane, the rapid chatter of their hooves echoing from all sides.

Eleanor peered up, keeping a sharp eye for the birds. The ravens tracked the fleeing party in a ragged flock from above, occasionally ducking lower to see their quarry through obstructions and cawing for the others to catch up.

Old Ryce took a series of tight turns deep into the warren of Ablerhyll, the alley darkening as the upper levels of the houses grew closer and closer together, blocking out the sky. Occasionally one of the people or a horse slipped in the muck underfoot, but none of them fell, and even as the smell of filth and refuse rose up to choke them, the birds became scarcer, unable to get through the overhanging rooftops, upper stories, washing lines, and bird nets hung by pigeon hunters.

"This way," called Old Ryce over his bony shoulder. "Nearly there!"

Through the narrowest of gaps between two lurching, irregular balconies that almost met above his head, Odo caught sight of the spire with the strange windmill. The blades were turning sluggishly in a faint wind, each lined with metal chimes, so the entire construction made a constant racket as it rotated, the same racket that Odo had noted earlier. The birds that hadn't been put off yet were scattered for good now, retreating with a series of indignant cries from the incessant metallic noise and the four giant blades threatening to smash them into a cloud of feathers.

"Through here," said Old Ryce, opening a large double door at the rear of the structure and waving them inside. Once they were all under cover, he dropped a bar down to seal the doors with an echoing slam.

The base of the spire was as big as a barn, with a high, arched ceiling and walls covered in mysterious pipes and gears leading up into the shadows. Over the sound of the chimes came a steady, mechanical clanking and gurgling. The horses whinnied nervously, and Eleanor sheathed Runnel in order to soothe hers by patting it on the neck as she caught her breath.

Egda's expression was pained, the sounds clearly an affront to his sensitive hearing. "What is this cacophonous place?"

"Ah! This is the answer to Sir Eleanor's question. What is Old Ryce doing here? Well, when he was released by the real dragon, who thankfully didn't take offense at the making of a fake one, he didn't know where to go, so he went where things needed fixing. First an axle on a wagon that broke in a ditch. Then a waterwheel with a wobble. Then a village clock that was stuck at midnight. Finally, this. Honest work!"

"I don't doubt it," said Hundred, dismounting, closely followed by the others. "But what is it?"

"A backward weather vane, Your Honor. Ain't it marvelous?"

"A weather vane that runs backward?" asked Odo. "What for?"

"Good question. You really ought to ask the clever chap who built it, only he's dead now. No one really knows how that happened — they found his shoes in a mud puddle in the cellar but nothing else — or understands the machine, but I can fix what seems to be broken. Indeed, I think I *have* fixed it, at long last. Funny how things don't seem to stay fixed around here. But all Old Ryce has to do now is pull the lever and see if it works."

"How will you know?"

"It'll rain. That's what it does. It brings rain to wash out the streets and feed the farms . . . and whatever else rain does."

Eleanor understood then. Ordinary weather vanes measured the weather. A backward weather vane *created* the weather. Remembering the dry fields on the way to Ablerhyll, she could well understand why the town would want one.

"Such devices were known of old," said Egda heavily. "But they were prohibited, with good reason. Interfering with weather is all too like the craft-workers who twist and change good animals into beasts like bilewolves."

"The Instrument hired me himself," said Old Ryce nervously. "Have I done wrong? Old Ryce means no harm, but if this is like that dragon engine —"

"Let us not be distracted by talk of the device," interrupted Hundred. "We are now trapped. How are we to escape Ablerhyll with ten horses in tow? We cannot leave them behind. We need them to get to the capital quickly."

"We are safe here for the moment," observed Runnel. "The birds cannot get in."

"The fiend who lit the craft-fire will be seeking other beasts even as we speak," said Biter. "One of us should go on a sortie to seek the smoke and deal with him once and for all."

"Craft-fires don't smoke — it all goes into the creatures they control," said Hundred. "But a sortie, all of us riding out at once, might work, if the gate is opened by someone first. I can sneak — wait, what's that?"

Over the ringing of the chimes and the clanking of the backward weather vane, they heard one dog howl, then another. Soon a whole pack was raising up an unnatural chorus.

"From birds to dogs," said Hundred grimly. "Even if the birds have lost us, the dogs will sniff us out."

"We can fight them off," said Eleanor. "Old Ryce, do you have any weapons?"

The old man looked fearfully around. "Just tools. And my lunch, Your Honors. But I want to help . . ."

"If we're going to make a stand here," said Odo, "it'd be better if you got out while you still can. This isn't your fight."

"Old Ryce has to help his friends. That's what friends do. Particularly when it's his fault they found you."

"It's not your fault," Eleanor said. "It's not Odo and me they're looking for. You just got caught up in this by accident."

"Indeed, and I will not have another innocent life on my conscience," said Egda. "Old Ryce, in the name of the authority I once bore, I command you to leave immediately."

"Authority?" echoed Old Ryce, blinking at Egda. "Command? Oh my, that nose . . . I thought I recognized it, but never dreamed . . ."

He went down on both knees, joints cracking loudly, and prostrated himself.

"Get up and run, man," said Hundred. "Before it's too late!"

Outside, the dogs fell silent, only to be followed a moment later by a heavy pounding on the huge doors.

"Open! Open!" boomed a voice. "By order of Instrument Umblewit!"

Oh dear," said Old Ryce, raising his eyes.

"Get rid of them," Hundred hissed. Old Ryce nodded and went to the gate, putting his head close to the bar.

"G-go away!" he shouted. "I'm busy!"

"Too busy for Instrument Umblewit? Don't forget who pays you, tinkerer."

"Um, Old Ryce is conducting a dangerous experiment. Oh, yes, very dangerous!"

"It'll be very dangerous for you if you don't let us in right now," came the retort, followed by renewed pounding. Fortunately, the doors were extremely solid and sounded as though they could take anything short of a battering ram.

"What can we do?" asked Eleanor. "We can't fight the entire town, can we?"

"We can fight our way through," said Hundred, testing her sword's edge with one thumb.

"Why don't we try to talk to them?" Odo asked, seeking another way. They had barely begun their mission and here they were facing certain death at the hands of the Instrument and his minions! "They're not really going to attack two knights, are they?"

"They will once they see us," said Hundred. "I am sure the orders have gone out to kill anyone who happens to be blind and has an impressive nose."

Egda's expression soured at that description, but he said nothing to contradict it.

"There has to be *something* we can do," said Eleanor, gripping Runnel tightly in frustration.

"There is a way out," said a pale-skinned, child-sized figure that stepped out of the deepest shadows, flanked by two just like it, but taller. It had green hair the color of an old bottle, and skin so thin that silvery veins could be seen pulsing beneath. Long fingernails tapped a stone-encrusted belt keeping its dark smock clinched about its waist. Black eyes regarded them with wary and not entirely welcoming calm.

"Urthkin!" barked Biter, jerking into a guard position.

"Where did you come from?" asked Odo, tugging his sword back down to his side. They had met these underground creatures before, and he remembered very well how dangerous they could be if provoked.

"From the earth," it told him, as though he had asked a stupid question.

"Stone make you strong," said Egda. "Darkness clear your sight."

The ritual greeting seemed to please the urthkin. "Wide be your halls. Tunnels guide you true."

The others joined Egda, bowing deeply to make themselves look as small as possible. Among the urthkin, height was deemed a disadvantage.

"What are you doing here, Urthkin?" asked Odo.

"The earth will offer you safe haven," the urthkin told Eleanor, who was the smallest, "if you agree to our terms."

"And, uh, what are your terms?" she asked.

"This machine must be destroyed."

"No!" Old Ryce exclaimed. "That is . . . dark ones . . . why? I don't even know if it works!"

The urthkin leader glanced at Old Ryce, whose head bobbed at a point significantly higher than hers, and again did not reply directly.

"We have tried to ruin this abomination many times," it told Eleanor. "Always, we have failed. The knowledge of its making and breaking is beyond us, and its key parts lie too high from the earth. But it is not beyond the tall one here." Another contemptuous glance at Old Ryce. "If he will end its terror, we will help you escape this place."

"Terror?" echoed Old Ryce, his mouth hanging open. "Has Old Ryce done it again? But there are no dragons this time . . . I promised!"

Eleanor soothed him. She didn't really know what was going on, but she recognized an opportunity for escape when she saw one.

"Could you destroy the machine if you had to?" she asked him. "Would you, if it was hurting someone?"

"Well, yes. But all it does is make rain. If it does. It hasn't been tested —"

"We know of such things from long ago," the urthkin told Eleanor. "And the tall one believes."

"Old Ryce does think it will work," said Old Ryce slowly. "Old Ryce has labored very hard, has puzzled out many strange things, has done work such has not be seen for —"

Clearly it mattered to the old man whether he had succeeded or failed.

"It must be destroyed," pronounced the urthkin.

A louder pounding on the door suggested those outside had found a battering ram of some kind.

"I suggest a fair trade," said Egda over the sound of the ram slamming into the door. "Let Old Ryce start the backward weather vane, but not let it continue very long, to see if it works. Rain will also distract our enemies outside, gaining us time."

"Does it work like that?" asked Eleanor to Old Ryce. "I mean, if you stop it and then destroy it, the rain will also stop?"

"Yes, yes," replied Old Ryce. "Little rain, then more rain, then lots more rain."

"How about a little rain, just for a few minutes, to see if it works, and then Old Ryce will destroy it," Eleanor proposed to the urthkin.

"Very little rain," said the urthkin.

"Yes, not too much," she told it, wondering why that was so important. "Old Ryce will wreck it once the skies open — isn't that right, Old Ryce?"

The old man nodded.

"And then you can show us how we can escape," she said. "How the earth can save us."

The urthkin inclined its head, but only minutely. "On my name, Shache, I swear it as scortwisa of Ablerhyll, scortwisa-that-was of Anfyltarn."

Eleanor blinked in surprise, understanding the urthkin term for leader. "You recognize me?"

"Yes, and your champion." Shache didn't glance at Odo, but he knew it meant him. The duel he had once fought and very nearly lost against an urthkin still haunted him.

"Is that why you helped us?" Eleanor asked.

"No." Shache bowed. "Proceed. Remember, very little rain. Too much, and we will leave you to your enemies. Or slay you ourselves, as oathbreakers."

Old Ryce glanced at Eleanor, and then at Egda. They both nodded, so he scampered off to a bank of levers and counterweights that occupied an entire wall. Grabbing the largest lever, he pulled with all his might.

When it failed to move, Odo joined him and added his considerable strength to the endeavor.

With a slow grinding noise, the lever came down, down, down, and then locked into its lowest position with a definite click, followed by a sound like thousands and thousands of bees buzzing inside the walls, a sound that slowly faded upward.

Old Ryce stepped back and looked around, rubbing his hands eagerly. "Hee hee, now we see."

"What's going on in there?" bellowed the voice from outside.

"Stand back!" Old Ryce called. "Big experiment about to begin!"

Even as he spoke, the backward weather vane was picking up speed, growing noisier with every second. Potent oils bubbled through pipes. Wooden cogs spun faster and faster, until they began to smoke. Dust rained down from far above, where the axle driving the four blades turned, rapidly becoming a blur.

Odo gathered the reins of two wide-eyed horses in each fist, stopping them from rearing in fright, the others restraining their horses too. The entire structure shuddered so violently around them that it seemed likely to collapse. There was nowhere within to take shelter.

"Is it working?" Eleanor asked Old Ryce, shouting over the deafening roar of machines. He was grinning like a madman.

"Let's find out!"

He tugged her to the base of a long pipe that snaked up to the very top of the spire and pressed her eye against it. Through it, via a series of cunning lenses, she saw the sky above. It was no longer blue. Thick, black clouds were gathering.

Even as she watched, a bolt of lightning leaped from one cloud to another with a sudden roar of thunder loud enough to drown out the backward weather vane.

Old Ryce clapped his hands and performed a capering dance.

"Any rain yet?" bellowed Hundred into Eleanor's ear.

She shook her head.

"Wait for the rain. It'll put out the craft-fire."

Eleanor pressed her eye back to the tube, understanding now why Egda had insisted on that particular condition. The urthkin might have driven a stiffer bargain had they known the humans were to gain more than just a simple distraction from the shower. It was so dark outside now that an urthkin wouldn't have been troubled by the sun. The pounding on the door had ceased as people looked skyward in wonder, waiting to see what would happen next.

No less than three lightning bolts cracked at once, and the deluge began.

With a deep-throated roar, torrential rain began to pour on Ablerhyll. Heavy drops fell on roofs and dripped through the spire's ancient eaves. Long trickles snaked under the barn doors, approaching the hooves of the nervous horses. The air smelled dense and heavy with moisture, and of a stranger tang, like lightning itself.

"Enough." A tiny, sharp-clawed hand gripped Eleanor's shoulder.

"Not yet," said Hundred. "A few more seconds."

"Enough!" declared Shache after the briefest of pauses, its black eyes following a particularly thick rivulet across the floor.

"Yes!" declared Eleanor. "Old Ryce, make it stop — for good!"

The aged mechanist stopped dancing midstep, looked sad for an instant, then nodded. Crossing once more to the bank of controls, he pulled several more levers and turned the screws on two wide pipes open to maximum. Then he stood back, dusting his hands on his tunic.

"What'll that do?" asked Odo.

"Make it go faster," said Old Ryce, looking up nervously. "Until it tears itself apart."

"How long?" asked Eleanor.

"About a minute."

"Then I think it's time you met your side of the bargain," Hundred told Shache. "Or we'll all die together."

"The earth will save us," said the urthkin. It walked several paces away and slapped the ground with its hands.

There was a rumble beneath their feet, the horses shifting nervously, and then the earth fell away to reveal a wide tunnel that sloped down into darkness.

The urthkin went ahead, a pale glow emanating from its skin, just enough for the humans to see the way.

"Let's go!" said Eleanor, ushering her horse forward. It needed little encouragement, spooked by all the noise above. One by one the party led their steeds into the welcome dark and quiet, even as the rainmaking machine behind them began to shudder itself to pieces.

Odo had never been so deep underground before. All around him he felt the weight and pressure of stone and earth. It was like nighttime, only a thousand times darker, save for the faint glimmer of the urthkin's skin ahead and a little light from the room behind. It was noisy, though, very noisy, with the footfalls of many people, plus ten horses, plus the racket of the backward weather vane echoing from the surface.

However the urthkin had opened the ground, it closed up behind them, just as the last packhorse made it in. With that sealing off went the very last of the lantern light from the chamber. A minute later, the ground shook and there was a terrific bang from above, the sound of the giant machine rending itself from top to bottom, the pieces falling in on themselves. It sounded like the world ending. Odo stopped for a full ten seconds with his hands over his head, half expecting the ceiling of the tunnel to collapse. Old Ryce stood over him with his hands pressed upward against the stone, as though prepared to hold it in place single-handedly.

The ceiling held, but the sound of small impacts echoed through the tunnel for some time. He hoped no one had been hurt. When it was over, Old Ryce sighed and sadly let his hands fall.

"There can't be anything of the spire left up there," said Eleanor in awe.

"Good," said Hundred. "They'll think us dead, crushed under the wreckage."

"Hurry," said Shache. "This road will not remain here long."

"What is this place?" asked Eleanor as the procession got moving again. Blinking, she realized in amazement that even though there were no obvious lights, she could still see. As well as the urthkin themselves, there were thin veins of moon-white light snaking through the stone walls, where something like fungus grew. The light was just enough to make out the shapes of those around her, so she could avoid stepping on anyone's toes, or being trodden on herself.

"You are in our lands . . . you have no words," the urthkin answered. "It is the home we have beneath your human home. An undercity, perhaps?"

"You mean you live down here?" asked Odo in horror. His words emerged as a choked squeak. Although he had known the urthkin lived in the earth, he had imagined vast caverns big enough to hold entire villages, not this narrow tunnel that wouldn't be here long.

"We live in many places," said Shache enigmatically. "Many of them are unknown to humans, who are forbidden here, just as we are forbidden in your cities."

"The ancient pact that has existed between urthkin and humans for hundreds of years allows urthkin to build under our towns whenever they like," Egda explained. "For the purposes of trade, mainly. It benefits both sides."

"We would never break that pact," Shache told them, "but humans sometimes do. Humans like Instrument Umblewit."

A strange sound echoed along the tunnel, that of many sets of urthkin teeth grinding together. Eleanor looked back and was surprised to see more than a dozen urthkin bringing up the rear.

Shache continued. "A foolish man brought the device that is now destroyed to Instrument Umblewit, hoping for reward. He had found it, hidden away, with a book that told of its use. Including how the machine could bring drenching rains — not to clean the streets or water the fields, but to drown urthkin, to flood us out of our under-city. This is what Umblewit threatened, because we would pay her no taxes, would not obey her commands to bring gold and gems and precious things of the earth. We, who have only ever brought prosperity to Ablerhyll in fair trade! If we could have slain her, we would have, but she is too cautious, too well guarded. We could only attempt to harm the lower parts of the machine."

"It was you!" exclaimed Old Ryce out of the darkness. "You're the reason the machine kept breaking down! Umblewit was going to punish me if I couldn't get it to work!"

"The urthkin had a right to defend themselves, since that device was intended as a weapon," said Egda, which seemed to Odo a fair summary of the injustice of the situation.

Old Ryce harrumphed a couple of times, as though he had something caught at the back of his throat, but a couple of solid pats on the back from Eleanor soon cleared the obstruction.

"We have many machines in the undercity," said Shache. "Machines for the digging of tunnels and seeking of gems. Perhaps the tall one would like to see them?"

Eleanor couldn't see Old Ryce well enough, but she could imagine the look of delight that crossed his face.

"The tall one would like that very much!" he exclaimed.

"It shall be so," said Shache.

They came to a junction in the tunnel. Odo could hear echoes vanishing off into two directions ahead, and even though he still wasn't breathing properly, he could tell that the air from the one to the left was much fresher than that to the right.

"Here we part ways," Shache told them. "Follow the tunnel that leads upward and it will open on a hillside out of sight of humans . . . *other* humans. The tall one will come with us, if he so wills. We will collapse the tunnel behind you."

The party split into two unequal parts, and the urthkin made moves to head on their way, deeper into the earth.

"Wait," said Egda. "Umblewit has broken the pact here, and perhaps others have done so elsewhere, but I would see it fixed in Ablerhyll and throughout the kingdom. You have my oath that everyone who suffers at the unjust hands of the Instruments will receive recompense."

"With darkness comes wisdom." Shache bowed. "I see that it is so with you, old one. Tunnels guide you true."

"Good-bye, Old Ryce!" called Eleanor. "Until we meet again!"

"Good-bye!" Odo managed to squeak out. He really didn't like being all closed in. Glowing urthkin veins and thin lines of mold on the walls simply did not compare with a well-trimmed lantern — or, even better, the bright sun.

"Good-bye! Good-bye!" echoed back to them from Old Ryce, and then they were alone.

The urthkin were as good as their word, as Odo had known they would be — a fact that gave him great comfort as they proceeded up the twisting, turning tunnel, leading the horses behind them. Within half an hour, there was a hint of greenish sunlight ahead, and then they were suddenly outside, in a stand of dense bushes that hid the tunnel opening from sight. Stepping through the bushes, Odo took a deep breath of deliciously fresh air and reacquainted himself with the vistas of the surface world. The sky was heavy with clouds and the ground damp underfoot, but the rain had ceased with the destruction of the backward weather vane and the air was still.

Hundred looked at the sun and declared them slightly south of the road they had intended to follow from Ablerhyll. Despite the turns and winding of the tunnel, they hadn't ultimately strayed far from their path.

"The sun is setting, sire," Hundred told her liege. "I would argue for traveling by night, but all are weary, the beasts no less than us. Perhaps a short respite is in order?"

"You are right, Hundred." The former king wearily inclined his head. He had been perfectly spry during their troubles in Ablerhyll, but now seemed once again to show his age. "We will make camp until moonrise, then continue on our way along the road, for that will be fastest."

"Why *does* he call you 'Hundred'?" Eleanor asked as they tethered the horses and began unloading them. She had often asked herself this question, wondering if it was perhaps the number of battles the old warrior had been in, or the number of people she had killed in battle, or the number of ways she knew how to kill people . . . or some other grisly fact entirely, as befitted a warrior of Hundred's experience.

"I come from a large family" was all Hundred said on the matter that night, before giving Eleanor a long list of chores to ensure she was too busy to ask again.

"Why is she always so mean to us?" Eleanor grumbled under her breath as she and Odo hurried to complete their tasks before darkness fell. "Aren't we knights too?"

"I like her," said Odo, although he mainly just liked knowing what he had to do. Being a knight had often felt like stumbling around in the dark, trying not to break anything valuable, and it came as a great relief to be told how to behave. Mostly, though, he was glad to be no longer underground — that was something he hoped never to have to endure again. "We're apprentice guards," he added. "It's our job to be bossed around."

"Many great knights have begun their lives as apprentice guards," said Biter. "Sir Winchell, for instance, spent a year emptying latrines before slaying the Vile Beast of Esceanda —"

"The two tasks were not unrelated," said Runnel. "One lived in the other."

"But the fact remains, sister: All must begin their journey somewhere."

"*Swords* don't start out at the bottom," Eleanor complained, then snickered at her unintended joke. "Like Sir Winchell did. You're just made . . . and enchanted . . . and off you go to see the world. I wish I could be like that."

"We are more than metal and magic," Runnel told her. "We learn just as you do."

"By our deeds are we known," Biter added with some finality, suggesting that the time for idle chat was over. "As are true knights."

Odo sensed that there was a lot more to the story of the swords than this. He knew little about how Runnel and Biter had been forged — but how much did he himself really know about how he had come to be? His father had told him bedtime stories as a young child about the courtship between him and his mother, but they were surprisingly light on details.

"Every day, we see something new," he reminded Eleanor, thinking of backward weather vanes, urthkin tunnels, and bespelled ravens.

"Yes, but it would be better if we were learning new things as well," she grumbled, disinclined to be satisfied.

Finally, the horses were cared for and the camp was prepared for the night. Odo and Eleanor wearily reclined on their bedrolls and listened to Egda and Hundred once again pursue a brief exchange with people who weren't there, including two whose names they had not heard before. Odo wondered how long until they started repeating their lost friends, and whether it made either of them any happier.

Hearing Egda and Hundred talk to the dead made Eleanor feel surrounded by ghosts lurking in the shadows. She shivered.

"Your education proceeds apace, my young knights," Egda told them, returning to the living with a scratch of his proud nose. Eleanor wondered if he had overheard her complaint about not learning anything. "My father always said that nothing compares to putting a person right into the affairs they wish one day to manage. 'Errors made in ignorance are lessons always learned,' he liked to tell me. At this pace, you will surpass Hundred and me in wisdom before you are half our age."

Warmed by the encouragement, Odo felt bold enough to ask something that had been on his mind all evening.

"This pact between humans and urthkin . . . who started it?"

"Ah, that would be Acwellen the Sage, many kings ago. He brokered a peace after a long history of squabbling between our two very different peoples. It turned out that, provided certain provisions were made regarding trade, we really had very few reasons to fight, except for occasional acts of pigheadedness on either part. It saddens me that we are in such a time at present."

"What will happen if the pact is permanently broken?" asked Eleanor, not wanting to fight the urthkin but thinking of the many battles — and the demand for brave knights — that might arise if it was.

"War," confirmed Hundred, the gleam of long-ago fires in her eyes.

"It will not come to that," said Egda. "Not while I live."

Odo had his doubts as to how much four people could do against the entire might of the regent and her Instruments, Adjustors, and Regulators, but he had faith in his betters, as he had been raised to, and suppressed his misgivings for now. Presumably the former king had allies he could call on, or at least favors to call in.

"Are there pacts with any other creatures?" he asked.

"Many," Hundred said in her brisk way, for Egda had fallen abruptly silent again, as was his wont at night. "Dragons, for instance."

"There's a pact with *dragons*?" Eleanor asked.

"Of course. Otherwise they might have eaten us all long ago." Hundred stood. "I'm going to cast about to see if anyone is looking for us from Ablerhyll. I won't be long. Swords, keep watch, and knightlings, rest, for we ride again in three hours."

"Yes, sir," said Odo and Eleanor as their enchanted swords took up position at either end of the camp.

Eleanor tried to calm her thoughts, but they were busy from the day and what lay ahead. She was beginning to appreciate that she occupied a small place in a very strange world full of very strange things, but that only made her want to see it all.

"Who do you think negotiated the pact with the dragons?" she asked Odo. "I wonder how it works."

But her friend was already asleep, and the swords didn't answer either. Soon, lulled by the chirruping of a nearby cricket or perhaps a lone, lost bat, she was asleep as well.

They rode all that night and slept the next day, granted a reprieve from all but the most basic of chores as they raced the sun to form a camp. There was no conversation that morning, just grateful collapse into sleep for all but Hundred, who took the first watch. Odo was next, and he was not easy to rouse. Knowing that Eleanor was tired, he gave her an extra hour before waking her up in turn.

"No troubles?" she yawned.

"Three bees," he told her. "But luckily your snoring scared them away."

"Ho ho. Get some rest, Jester Knight, or I'll let the bees sting you when they come back."

Eleanor perched on a log near Runnel, rubbing her eyes and wishing there was a fire so she could make some tea. This was the worst part of being a knight, she thought, sitting around waiting for something to happen. And when something *did* happen, it was often horrible and entirely out of her control. She had greatly preferred it when she and Odo had been off on their own adventures, answerable to only themselves, even though there were times the errors she'd made in ignorance had very nearly cost her life or the lives of others. At least back then she hadn't been expected to do chores all day and dig other people's toilets and ride until she ached in every joint.

Still, it was better than staying at home and doing nothing. Of that she was completely certain. She was seeing the world, albeit slower than she would have liked. And every now and again Egda let something slip about the life in court that awaited them.

The sun sank slowly toward the horizon, painting the western sky in brilliant reds and oranges. Her instructions were to wake the others when the fiery disc touched the distant hills. As the shadows lengthened, she thought she heard the high-pitched cries of the lost bat again, but she put it out of her mind in order to do as she had been instructed.

"Hundred?" she said, shaking the old woman's shoulder. This time the warrior had both eyes closed, properly asleep. "Time to wake up."

The next thing Eleanor knew, she was on her back with a glittering knife at her throat. Then Hundred's eyes cleared and she came fully awake, letting Eleanor go with a grunt. She stood up and replaced the knife into a pocket at her side in one fluid movement.

Behind her, floating in the air like a giant silver mosquito with an emerald eye, hovered Runnel, caught between saving her knight and respecting Eleanor's superior.

"That can be tonight's first lesson," Hundred told Eleanor, who got nervously to her feet and brushed herself down, feeling as though a dozen small rocks had embedded themselves through her tunic into the skin of her back.

"Let sleeping knights lie, or at least rouse them gently, if you want to see another sunset."

"Yes, sir."

"Get the other knightling to his feet and we'll start on your next lesson . . . if I haven't put you off?"

Eleanor nodded, face burning. Hundred too had obviously heard her complaint about not learning anything. She would have to mind her tongue more carefully.

"Do not be despondent," whispered Runnel as she returned to Eleanor's side. "I for one relish the chance to learn alongside the great knight you will undoubtedly become, unlike the others I have served."

But it wasn't combat Hundred taught them, it was how to scratch together a healthy breakfast from roots and berries found in the copse nearby, supplemented by insects attracted to the light of a small fire. Boiled and mashed together with a small amount of water, then fried as a paste on a blackened iron plate, the mixture was not nearly as revolting as either Eleanor or Odo feared. In fact, it had an almost-pleasant nutty taste and left them feeling full and energized for the night ride ahead.

"There's a bat flapping around the camp," commented Odo as they packed up. "I've seen it fly over three times in the last minute."

"How can you tell it's the same one?" Eleanor asked.

"It's small, but really fast. Like a mouse with wings." Not at all like the legendary barrow bats, which were rumored to be as fat as rats, with wingspans as long as his arm. He was glad it wasn't one of those. "Do you think the same person who sent the bilewolves and ravens sent this one too?"

"I've never heard of craft-workers using bats," said Eleanor. "What can we do about it anyway?"

"I'll tell Hundred," said Odo. "Best to be careful."

Eleanor forgot about the bat as Odo wandered away to talk to Hundred, and focused on reviewing strikes and blocks. If she wasn't going to learn anything new, she would at least remember everything she'd learned already.

They rode quickly, following Hundred with Egda safely protected between them. The sky was clear, with stars so bright it seemed sometimes they were about to fall. When the moon rose, it was half full, and painted the road with ripples of light. The horses made a driving, percussive rhythm as the party climbed steadily higher in altitude, broaching the shoulders of a mountain range that Hundred called the Offersittan, which stood as a barrier directly across their path.

"The usual way to cross the Offersittan is at Kyles Frost," she said as they dismounted to walk the horses for a while, before changing to the fresher ones. "However, that will be impossible for us because it is closely guarded. When you see the twin peaks Twisletoth and Tindit standing on the horizon like the horns of a giant beast, you will know that we are close and need to be wary of other travelers on this road."

"Do you have a plan?" Eleanor asked.

"Perhaps to go around it, although that will take us much longer. I believe in preserving all possibilities, as long as my name is Hundred . . . Ah! Our stealthy companion has made its move at last!"

The bat had dropped out of the sky with a leathery flapping and grasped a branch directly overhead, emitting an impatient series of squeaks and chirps. It was thin and shivering, as though very weak.

A small throwing knife appeared in Hundred's hand. Runnel and Biter joined their knights as all three of them took up positions around Egda, who asked, "What is it? Another bird attack? But this sounds different."

"It's a bat," said Eleanor. "And it's been following us."

With so many blades pointing at it at once, the little creature squawked back into the air and resumed circling.

"It was searching for us the night we escaped Ablerhyll," said Hundred, who had not needed Odo's warning, "and found us this morning. I have watched it closely ever since, awaiting a third approach from our enemy, the lighter of the craft-fires, but there has been no sign of any other animal adversaries. I believe that this is something different. No less a threat, perhaps, but not of an immediate nature."

"What made it land now?"

"I believe, Sir Eleanor, it was because I said my name."

The bat flapped around them three times, occasionally coming closer, then darting away. It was indeed very small, and presented no obvious danger to them. Eleanor was sure Hundred could have downed it with a knife, and as she hadn't, was forced to conclude that Hundred intended more from the encounter than a swift end to the creature.

"Let it approach," Egda told them. "If its intentions

are perfectly natural, or at least peaceful, we will soon know. Perhaps our enemy wishes to treat with us."

"Aye, sir." Hundred lowered her hand to her side, but kept the blade at the ready. Odo and Eleanor did the same.

The bat circled one more time, then swooped in to grasp the same branch as before. Gripping the tree tightly and tucking its wings against its sides, it regarded them from its upside-down position with eyes as black as jet.

"Its eyes aren't smoky," said Eleanor. "It's not some craft-worker's servant."

The bat's ugly muzzle twitched as it started squeaking again.

"Sounds like it's talking to us," said Odo.

"But bats can't talk, can they?" Eleanor, cocking an ear, could make no sense of the string of tiny sounds. "Not like dragons."

"What's it doing?" asked Hundred. "Talking, you say?"

"Can't you hear it?" Odo glanced at the puzzled face of Hundred and knew his answer.

"I hear nothing," said Egda. "The pitch of its voice must be too high for my old ears."

"I hear it, but can make no sense of it," said Odo slowly.

"𝓘 𝓱𝓮𝓪𝓻 𝓷𝓸𝓽𝓱𝓲𝓷𝓰," said Biter with a puzzled shiver.

"Listen," said Eleanor, concentrating hard. "It almost sounds like . . . like letters . . ."

Odo frowned. She was right. The tiny bat wasn't saying words, but spelling them!

"— r! y! k! u! r! g! e! s! h! a! s! t! e! p! r! i! n! c! e! k! e! n! d! —"

"What's it saying?" Eleanor said. "I can't string it together quickly enough."

"I can," said Odo. "Hang on."

His mouth moved as he followed the rapid stream of letters, supplying spaces and punctuation where they seemed likely to fit. Soon, he found that the bat was repeating one message over and over.

" 'Prince Kendryk urges haste,' " he said. "It's a message from Prince Kendryk!"

"From the heir himself!" said Egda. "Even as a boy, my great-nephew had an unusual bond with animals, and kept many pets."

"Wait." Odo held up a hand. "The letters have changed."

"I'm getting it now." Eleanor listened closely. "The message says, 'Imprisoned. My coronation canceled. Regent to be crowned king. Only the old dragon can save Tofte now.' Who's the old dragon?"

"My king," said Hundred to Egda, who huffed impatiently. "He means you. Kendryk must indeed have sent this missive."

The bat fell silent, message delivered in full, and watched each of them closely as they spoke, enormous ears seeming to take in every word. Its strange features were screwed up in a state of permanent anxiety, and Odo felt a pang of sympathy for it. This poor animal had flown all the way from Winterset, across mountains and plains, probably lost them in Ablerhyll because of the underground tunnel, then found them a day ago only to be unsure who they were until it heard Hundred's name. This wasn't a message that could fall into the wrong hands, after all.

"Do you have a name?" Odo asked it, wishing he had a bug or something to offer it.

"t! i! p!"

"Tip?"

"m! i! s! s! e! d! t! h! e! c! a! v! e! m! o! u! t! h! b! y! a! w! i! n! g! t! i! p!"

"Tip will do." Odo reached a hand up to where the bat clung to the branch. It eyed him warily for a moment, then stepped across like an inverted parrot. Its feet were sharp-tipped and clung tightly to him, but not painfully because it was feather-light. It was shivering less now, as though getting used to them.

"Well, you've always wanted a pet." Eleanor smirked.

"But now what do I do?" Odo asked, standing awkwardly while Tip looked trustingly up at him.

"Interrogate it while we ride," said Hundred. "Learn everything it knows. Then we will decide."

"But how . . . where do I put it?" He waved his arm back and forth. Tip's feet shuffled from side to side, maintaining their tight grip.

"Affix a scarf around your throat. Let it cling to that."

"It's a *him*, I think," Eleanor said, helping Odo with the scarf.

When the woolen collar was in place, he brought Tip closer and the bat swapped his grip.

"There, a bat necklace." Eleanor tickled Tip on the top of his head, which hung down almost to Odo's belly button. He blinked up at her and might have smiled. She found it hard to tell exactly what that ugly face was doing, but in manner he wasn't unfriendly.

"Mount up," said Hundred. "Let's away. If everything this creature tells us is true, we have even less time than we thought."

Odo found it hard to ride and follow Tip's spelled-out squeaking at the same time. Luckily his horse, once again the intelligent Wiggy, knew to follow Hundred's even when her rider was distracted. To make matters even more difficult, what Tip told him was filtered through the intelligence of a small bat, so much of it was about the moths that lived high above throne rooms and other meeting places, cracks that led to caves underneath the city, and which guards disliked bats to the point of trying to skewer them on pikes. Only where Prince Kendryk had instructed the bat specifically did he have information of use to another human.

One message was very clear: If the Old Dragon didn't appear in time, all would be lost.

"Why are you called the Old Dragon?" Eleanor asked Egda as they rode.

Hundred barked a laugh. "Be careful what you say, Sir Eleanor. He never liked the name, no matter how well earned."

The former king grimaced. "I was dubbed so upon defeating the giant Fylswingan of Brathanad — although truthfully, it is an inherited title, passed down along my line for three hundred years. Every king tends to earn it eventually, even the most placid."

"So Prince Kendryk will be the Old Dragon one day too?"

"Yes, if he is given the opportunity to become king in truth — and to grow old, as so many have been denied."

Egda descended into a funk, bringing the subject to a close.

They rode on as the road became ever steeper, winding through valleys and over ridges, past forests and beside rivers Eleanor had never heard of. Occasionally Tip launched himself from Odo's throat to seek out a tasty snack, but mostly he stayed in place, spelling out his messages and resting after his long flight.

"He says the regent's coronation is in three days," Odo told the others as they watered the horses in a stream and swapped mounts. "That's not enough time for us to get there, is it?"

"Not unless we travel day and night," said Egda. "Perhaps not even then."

"Or we cross the Offersittan at Kyles Frost," Hundred said.

"I thought you said we couldn't do that," said Eleanor. "It's too well guarded."

"I said it's impossible, not that we couldn't do it."

"Hundred eats the impossible for breakfast and hunts the inconceivable for supper," Egda commented with a weak smile. "As Beremus used to say."

Eleanor and Odo exchanged a glance. The dead were dead and likely to stay that way — unless talked about too much, as some in Lenburh believed. Though neither of the young knights believed this, they were a little alarmed when Egda and Hundred talked about their dead friends, particularly when Hundred assumed their voices.

"Is it only impossible to cross at Kyles Frost as ourselves?" asked Odo.

"𝔄 𝔡𝔦𝔰𝔤𝔲𝔦𝔰𝔢!" agreed Runnel eagerly. "𝔖𝔬𝔪𝔢𝔱𝔥𝔦𝔫𝔤 𝔪𝔬𝔯𝔢 𝔱𝔥𝔞𝔫 𝔣𝔞𝔨𝔢 𝔫𝔞𝔪𝔢𝔰."

"𝔒𝔯 𝔴𝔢 𝔠𝔬𝔲𝔩𝔡 𝔡𝔯𝔞𝔴 𝔱𝔥𝔢 𝔤𝔲𝔞𝔯𝔡𝔰 𝔞𝔴𝔞𝔶 𝔣𝔯𝔬𝔪 𝔱𝔥𝔢 𝔭𝔞𝔰𝔰," said Biter, "𝔴𝔦𝔱𝔥 𝔞 𝔰𝔭𝔢𝔠𝔱𝔞𝔠𝔲𝔩𝔞𝔯 𝔡𝔦𝔳𝔢𝔯𝔰𝔦𝔬𝔫. 𝔍𝔱 𝔴𝔬𝔲𝔩𝔡 𝔟𝔢 𝔢𝔞𝔰𝔶 𝔱𝔬 𝔞𝔯𝔯𝔞𝔫𝔤𝔢 𝔞𝔫 𝔞𝔳𝔞𝔩𝔞𝔫𝔠𝔥𝔢."

"Easy to get us all killed too, foolish sword," said Hundred, tapping her chin with one gloved finger. "Before we formulate any kind of plan, we must obtain information. On nearing Kyles Frost, we will send Tip ahead to scout for us. What he sees from the air will greatly aid us in our passage."

"Oh," said Odo. "I thought we'd send him back to Winterset with a message for the prince, so he knows we're coming."

He'd be safer there too, Odo thought to himself.

"Later, perhaps, but not now." Hundred dismissed that suggestion. "He is more use to us here. At this pace we will be close enough to put him to work by midnight or thereabouts tomorrow. Tip must be ready by then. The winds blow powerful and cold over the pass at all times."

"How did the king put the message in Tip and make him talk in the first place?" asked Eleanor. "Perhaps we could do the same to another bat, or an owl or something."

"It is a great skill," said Egda. "His father, Prince Aart of Gelflund, had the knack of it, and clearly he taught young Kendryk. I do not have that skill, and neither does Hundred. The only gift old soldiers like us have is experience."

"And plenty of it," said Hundred, mounting in one smooth motion. "Time passes. We must make a good distance yet before dawn, if we are to meet this new deadline. I see craft-fires and bilewolves in my waking dreams."

They mounted and rode off, trading potholes and low-hanging branches for the larger concerns waiting ahead.

TEN

Tip stayed at Odo's throat for the rest of the journey, blinking up at him with tiny black eyes and snuggling into the scarf for warmth. Odo quickly became accustomed to his presence and on occasion completely forgot he was there, particularly as the road wound like a snake around hills and along increasingly steep-sided valleys, requiring him to take more care with Wiggy's footing. They had long bypassed the town of Trumness, where Reeve Gorbold's pigeon had died, and were now entering the foothills of the Offersittan. The mountains themselves loomed like vast, black storm clouds directly before them.

Eleanor strained through the darkness to catch sight of the sentinels of the pass that led between Twisletoth and Tindit, vast stony fangs she had read about in accounts of the deeds of mighty knights. They were so high, it was said, that snow never melted at their summits, and ice trickling down their sides carried strange relics frozen many centuries ago.

Imagine, she thought, what it would be like to skate those ice rivers from the summit all the way down to the bottom. She was a good skater, having learned the two times in her life that the river had frozen over. What a thrill that would be!

Glancing behind him, Odo saw by moonlight that Eleanor was grinning, and wondered what new thought was running through her mind. There was always something. At least she was happy.

The strange sensation of a tiny bat burrowing into his throat and a series of small squeaks distracted him.

"What's that, Tip?"

"o! w! l! s!"

"Owls?"

"h! u! n! t! i! n! g! i! h! e! a! r! t! h! e! m!"

"Where? I can't see them."

"f! a! r!"

Tip burrowed even tighter into Odo's chest, as though trying to make himself invisible.

"Tip hears owls," Odo told the others, and Hundred immediately reined in her horse so he could tell her what he knew.

"Owls hunt bats," Eleanor said.

"And when directed by a craft-fire," Hundred said, "they might hunt people too. There are pale owls in the mountains, as big as large dogs. Quickly, head for that stand of trees."

They galloped under cover and tied the horses to the trunks, giving them an early feed to keep them quiet. Dawn wasn't far away; Eleanor could see it in the sky even with the mountains cloaking the eastern horizon. She stared westward, where she imagined any pursuit might originate, and within moments her attention was rewarded.

Two huge white birds, flapping in tandem, came into view. They flew high above the road, carefully following its tight-wound twists, heads turning from left to right to scan every inch. There was no doubt what they hunted. Or who.

"Quiet now." Hundred's instruction was barely a whisper of air.

Odo and Eleanor crowded into each other under the stand of trees, listening as flapping wings came closer, passed overhead, then went on up the road. Eleanor didn't realize how tightly she had been holding Runnel, or even that she had drawn her sword at all, until the owls had flown by them.

"Two more breaths, to be sure," Hundred instructed.

Odo counted three, then dared move again.

"Will they come back?" he asked.

"Not in full daylight," Egda said. "Our pursuer might use other birds, I suppose, but they do not know for certain that we are on this road, or we would have been assaulted in force. But we must be wary of any animals acting in concert or behaving strangely. Still, for now I think we will be safe to emerge from cover."

"Tip has proved his worth most handsomely," added Hundred. "Would that I had such sharp hearing!"

Odo tickled the bat between his enormous ears and Tip chittered ordinary bat noises in response.

"Dawn is upon us," Hundred said. "Let us make camp

here. Build no fire, knightlings. Even with Tip, we will take no chances."

The day passed slowly, the coldness of the air becoming apparent to all in their turns to sit watch. The sun, when it finally appeared over the crest of the mountains ahead, was weak and watery. A belly of cold provisions hardly helped.

Odo sat thinking with Tip curled up at his throat, sleeping as bats do naturally during daylight hours. Before turning in, he had listened to Egda and Hundred once again conversing with their fallen friends, and again found reason for disquiet. Honoring the dead was one thing; keeping grief and sorrow alive was quite another.

All through his watch, the last before waking the others to resume their journey, he pondered a plan to lay the past to rest. Once he had it, the question was only whether he had the courage to put it into effect.

"What weighs on your mind, Sir Odo?" asked Biter when he faltered in the middle of some quiet practice on the edge of the campsite. "Your strokes are heavy and your eye is off by a good yard. Were that tree a bilewolf, you would be torn asunder!"

"I wish I was more like Hundred," Odo said. "She doesn't have any doubts. I keep telling myself that I'm a real knight. That I, uh, eat adversity for an afternoon snack. But all I can think about is how things could go wrong, even when I know what I need to do."

"I am sure many things have gone wrong for my

knights in my past, although in truth I can't remember what they might have been," said Biter, slipping out of Odo's hand and coming around to face him, emerald flashing in the dappled light. "Knowing what one must do is the hardest lesson for some knights to learn. Though it is generally better to do something than nothing."

"For once my brother has wisdom," said Runnel, darting from Eleanor's side to join them. "What is it you know you must do, Sir Odo? Perhaps we can help you find the means."

He told them, which was a trial in itself, but they did not think him foolish or rash. It seemed mad to him to try to tell a former king what to do, but they did not think so.

For the rest of his watch they formulated a plan, and when it was time for Hundred and Egda to wake, they put it into effect.

"My liege, the sun is setting." Odo woke Egda first, knowing what had happened to Eleanor the previous day when she'd woken Hundred.

"Thank you, good knight." Egda sat and threw off his bedroll in one motion. He might already have been awake, for all Odo could tell. There was no way to know behind the blindfold whether his eyes were closed or open. "Today we ride in earnest."

"What is this?" asked Hundred, who had definitely been asleep a moment ago. She was on her feet, staring at the fruits of Odo's labor on the edge of the camp.

"I mean no disrespect," he said, nudging Eleanor's bedroll with his toe, not entirely sure which way up she was lying under it. No part of her was visible. "But there is something we must leave behind us. That is . . . I believe we ought to . . . if you agree, my liege . . ."

He executed a clumsy bow, hoping he wasn't making a grave mistake and overstepping himself.

"Speak, Sir Odo," said Egda.

"You were good to us in Lenburh," he went on. "We were grieving for Sir Halfdan as well as Bordan, Halthor, and Alia. You took charge and helped us put him to rest. That was a kindness we all needed. Now I think . . . that is, if you don't mind me saying . . . it's nothing to do with ghosts or the like, honest . . ."

"What the big stampcrab here is trying to tell you is that he'd like to do for you what you did for us," said Eleanor, struggling to her feet and quickly grasping the line of Odo's reasoning. "You've lost many people. Good people, and friends. You've been lamenting their loss in the wilderness for a long time. Maybe it's time to set down that task, now you're coming back into the world. There's no good in dragging the dead around when they haven't asked you to. They don't take kindly to it, or so the stories go."

Odo looked gratefully at his oldest friend, who always had words when he did not, even when she was only half-awake. He wondered if her father had told her something similar when her mother had died. "I thought we might . . . lessen your sadness. Not forget your friends, but let them rest."

The former king didn't respond. He looked older than ever, and his expression was impossible to read.

Odo glanced at Hundred, who inclined her head in the tiniest of nods.

"The lad has built a grave, sire," she told Egda in a soft voice. "There are twigs and berries — an old Karnickan ritual, I believe. A stick for the body, a seed for the soul? To put grief to rest and let the happy memories thrive?"

"That's right," Odo said.

"How did you — ?" A crack in Egda's voice prompted him to stop and clear his throat. "Of course. The good swords have been continuing their education of our young knights while our backs are turned."

Odo swallowed. "Are you angry, sire?"

"Not at you, and not for any of this. You are right. I must shed my present load in order that my shoulders can adopt another. You are my guide, Sir Odo. I place myself in your hands."

He held out his own hands and Odo took them gently, with utmost respect and kindness, and led the former king to the long trench he had dug, where they both knelt. The trench was a foot across, a foot deep, and four feet long. Biter and Runnel stood at one end with their sharp points in the soft earth. Two piles of twigs and berries lay next to the trench. Foraging for them while keeping a careful eye on the camp had taken Odo his entire watch.

"Take a twig in one hand and a berry in the other," he said, guiding Egda. "Say a name. Then Hundred will take the twig and Eleanor will take the berry. They'll put them in the hole, one by one. When we're done, I'll cover them all up and you can say a few words if you'd like to."

Egda nodded. Drawing a deep breath, he did as Odo instructed, clutching a twig and berry, one in each hand.

"Beremus," Egda said.

Eleanor and Hundred reached to take the berry and twig from his fingers. He resisted for an instant, then let go. Hundred snapped the twig and placed the pieces in the hole. Eleanor pressed the berry into the exposed soil, where it might release its seeds and grow.

"Beremus," they repeated, and Odo and the swords said the name too.

"Peg." Another twig, another berry.

"Peg."

"Sir Sutton."

"Sir Sutton."

So it went until the two piles had dwindled almost to nothing, and Odo began to wonder if he had gathered enough. How many close friends was it possible to lose in one lifetime? How had Egda borne so much grief for so long?

Finally, with just three twigs left, Egda raised shaking hands to the golden blindfold and slid it up and over his head, revealing red-rimmed, milky eyes. Tears trickled down his cheeks and gathered in the furrows at the corners of his mouth.

"I am done," he said.

Odo used his big hands like shovels to fill in the hole, and Eleanor and Hundred helped him pat it down, making a miniature barrow. Then they knelt back and waited in silence. It mattered to none of them that night had fallen and a strenuous journey awaited. Tip watched them with somber eyes, sensing that this was human business that he didn't need to understand and was best to stay out of.

"When I was king," Egda finally said, "I was surrounded by many who called me friend. I soon learned to recognize, and hold in the highest regard, those whose friendship was true. They are more rare and more precious than jewels. In the wilderness, I held their memories tightly, feeling that I was poorer for losing them than the entire wealth of the kingdom. Now I see that I was doubly a fool: a fool once for thinking a blind man cannot still be king, and a fool twice for thinking a man who has been rich in friends and lost them can never regain that wealth. Today, I am made fivefold richer, for now I have Hundred, and Sir Odo and Biter, and Sir Eleanor and Runnel. I thank you, friends, from a heart that beats stronger already."

They inclined their heads, Odo blushing furiously. He had expected Egda to talk about Beremus and the others, not about *him*.

"It was all Sir Odo's idea," Eleanor said. She didn't dare blink, for fear of releasing a tear from the fullness of her eyes. She was thinking of her mother and imagining how proud she'd be to know that a king had said such fine things to them. She also promised that she'd bury a twig and a berry for her and Sir Halfdan when she returned to Lenburh. It was a lovely thing to do.

"You do each other credit," said Egda, replacing the blindfold and rising resolutely to his feet. "And I have no doubt that you will return the honor at first opportunity, Sir Eleanor. Now, we must ride like the winds of Gelegestreon to reach the approach to Kyles Frost before sunrise. Spare no horses and give no quarter! Are you with me, knights?"

Odo and Eleanor leaped to their feet and swept up their swords.

"Yes, sire!"

Hundred made a show of rising more slowly. "Let's at least save some of the horses in the event we need them again. And perhaps we should pack up the camp first, before rushing off into the night? I for one would miss my bedroll."

Egda, a grave man who Eleanor and Odo had hardly ever seen smile before, amazed them both by roaring with laughter.

"The mighty Hundred, dragging her heels to enter the fray? Thought I'd never see the day!"

Pack up the camp they did, eating nuts and stale bread as they went, but when they mounted and set off, Egda riding close at Hundred's heels, it was all Eleanor and Odo could do to keep up.

It grew colder and colder, until Eleanor and Odo shrugged into the cloaks packed in Lenburh but never needed previously, and the steel of their swords grew icy to the touch. The horses' breath steamed as they strained up the ever-rising slope, while the foliage around them grew gnarly and stunted as if here even plants hunkered down against the chill.

The moon was behind them when they passed under a sleeping hamlet that grew out of a cliff wall like some strange forest fungus. Few candles flickered around tightly sealed shutters, but still the party of four, ten horses, two swords, and one bat slowed their pace to a stealthier trot and kept their faces carefully obscured.

No one halted them. Glancing over her shoulder at the hamlet receding into the night, Eleanor saw no sign that anything living had observed their passing.

The memory of the pale owls kept pace with her, however. She felt the gaze of their invisible master in the space between her shoulder blades like a physical pressure. It never slipped any of their minds that they were being hunted.

One hour before dawn, they pulled off the road into a sheltered alcove, a hollowed-out cave with just enough room for all of them.

"Before we proceed much farther along this road," Hundred told them, "we must determine what we face. It is time to send Tip on his mission."

The little bat stirred eagerly at the sound of his name. Odo held out his arm, and Tip walked along it until he could see all four of them equally well. The willingness of his expression touched Odo's heart. He had no doubt their new friend would do anything they asked — but what if there was an archer ahead the equal of the one that had killed Reeve Gorbold's pigeon over Trumness? What if a flock of ensorcelled owls tore him into tiny pieces?

Odo stilled his fears as Hundred gave the bat his instructions in the plainest possible terms. Tip was to fly along the road up to the pass, counting guards as he went. He was to note any archers and unusual animal behaviors as well. Then he was to fly back to them as quickly as possible. If he was seen aloft after dawn, their craft-fire-lighting pursuer might follow him to where Egda and the others awaited his return.

"y! e! s! y! e! s! y! e! s!"

The little bat nodded, which was a strange gesture to see upside down, then opened his wings and flew off, chirruping happily as he went. Odo hoped he would take the opportunity to eat some insects along the way. Hundred had said that the winds blowing over the pass were strong. He would need all his strength to survive them.

"Don't fret," said Eleanor, patting his shoulder. "Tip must have flown through the pass once already — on the way here, remember?"

"Oh, yes, of course." That did make Odo feel better.

He rubbed down Wiggy and swapped his saddle over to his second mount, the dun Salu. Hundred inspected his work with the horses, as she often did, and Eleanor's too. There was still much for them to learn about caring for the beasts. Until they had squires, they would have to look after their horses themselves, if they ever had horses of their own. That was assuming they survived the bitter chill in the air . . .

Winter in Lenburh wasn't half as cold as they felt they were that night, and Eleanor was for once grateful for the chores Hundred gave them. Even sheltered from the light predawn snow that settled on the valley road, and even with the body warmth of the horses around them, she was soon shivering. Seeing this, Odo loaned her a spare woolen hat that went over her own, and came down almost over her eyes. It helped, but she was too cold to stay still. The chores kept her moving, and moving kept her warm.

"Shame there's not enough room under here for us to practice," she said through chattering teeth. One swing of Runnel would likely cut two horses in half.

"Here, catch," said Hundred, taking something that glittered from behind her back and tossing it to her in an underarm throw.

It moved so quickly Eleanor didn't realize it was a knife until it was halfway into her hand. Only at the last instant did she twist and catch it by the handle — and only then did she see the tiny scabbard that protected the blade. Her fingers had never been in any danger.

"And here, one for you." A second blade crossed the distance to Odo. He fumbled with one hand, lunged with the other, and after a quick juggle finally snatched it out of the air. When he looked up, Hundred held two more knives, one in each hand, and Egda was grinning.

"Attack me," Hundred said. "Expose your blades if you wish. It will make no difference."

Odo didn't doubt that, but Eleanor was willing to accept the challenge. She had practiced for hours with one of her father's old scalpels, as blunt as a stick but well balanced and perfectly effective against the gnarled apple tree in her backyard back home. She dropped into a fighting crouch and inched forward, watching Hundred's hands. When she saw her chance, she lunged.

Hundred let her get close, then twisted on her heels and moved in such a way that left Eleanor disarmed and with a knife at her throat.

"You are dead," the old woman whispered into Eleanor's ear before letting her go. "Pick up your knife and try again."

Eleanor grinned and did as she was told. This was exactly what she had been waiting for!

Odo came to her aid, circling around so they were attacking Hundred from opposite sides. Again, however, Hundred repelled their lunges with dizzying ease.

"Now you are both dead."

Odo took that as both a caution and a challenge. "Any suggestions, Biter?"

"I fear my advice would be useless, Sir Odo."

"This is itself good advice," Egda said. "An enchanted sword can only teach you how to *defend* against a knife, using a sword. There is no such thing to my knowledge as an enchanted knife, so you must fight Hundred the hard way."

With that, Hundred lunged at Odo, but it was a feint, and a second later Eleanor was "dead" again, and Odo soon followed. Even though he tried hard just to stay alive, it was impossible to keep out of Hundred's reach. She was too nimble.

"Never suppose that sword and armor make you invulnerable," she told them. "One day you may be without either, and this lesson could save your life. Now watch closely and I will show you the disarm I used the first time."

Eleanor soaked up this new knowledge like Swithe the leatherworker soaked up his ale, not even noticing the cold anymore. In fact, she soon shrugged out of the cloak in order to free her arms, although she kept Odo's hat to spare her ears.

"Now, against each other." Hundred watched as the young knights sparred. The horses seemed to be watching too, or at least not shying away when the scuffle occasionally came near them. The small stable formed a ring around the two fighters, flicking their ears and tails as though in amusement.

"Enough," said Hundred finally. "It will be dawn soon. Best spare your strength for Tip's return."

Eleanor studied the knife as she handed it back to its owner. The blade was one she hadn't seen before, slender, with a grip worn into the shape of Hundred's fingers. There were no jewels or any other adornments on the blade, handle, or sheath. It was what it was: a well-made weapon that had seen a great deal of service.

"How many knives do you carry?" Eleanor asked. "I've counted at least eleven."

"That many?" asked Egda with an amused look. "Are you sure they're all different?"

"Yes," Eleanor said, listing all those she had seen since the fight against the bilewolves. "Plus the sword. There can't be many more or you'd jangle."

"I would indeed. And I would be very heavy." Hundred didn't smile, although that could have been a joke. "Weapons are tools. I like to keep one for every eventuality. Estimate the number of eventualities, and you will know the number of my blades."

A flutter of wings came from the opening of their shelter. They turned as one to see Tip flapping furiously. He emitted a series of excited calls on seeing them, and caught Odo's outstretched arm in a tight grip. Tip wrapped himself in his wings, shivered, and breathed heavily.

"Welcome back, little friend," said Odo, beaming in relief. "I was beginning to wonder."

"Well, I didn't doubt you for a second," Eleanor said, handing him a piece of dried fruit she had saved from supper. Tip gulped it down — or up, as the case was.

"Tell Sir Odo and Sir Eleanor what you saw," said Hundred. "All of it."

They crowded around to hear. Tip had a lot to spell out, and frequently he was asked to go back and repeat short passages where their interpretations differed. It soon became clear that a considerable force lay ahead of them, with thirty soldiers and six archers protecting the pass from every approach. The gates were closed and barred, and anyone nearing was stopped. A small camp had formed beside the road, temporary home to those who had been turned back. Rather than descend all the way back down, it appeared they were willing to wait until those the guards were looking for had arrived and been caught, and the gates opened again.

Odo's mood flagged as Tip's account came to its unhappy conclusion. There was no way through the pass that didn't involve a fight — a fight they were likely to lose, against such numbers . . . and archers too. At least they still had the advantage of surprise.

"Thank you, Tip," said Egda to the tiny creature. "You have served us well."

Tip wriggled with pleasure and burrowed into Odo's scarf, blinking exhaustedly.

"So what do we do now?" asked Eleanor. Even she was daunted by the odds. "Turn back and find another way around?"

"We press on," said Hundred. "All is not lost."

"Let us make a war council," said Biter, "while we camp here for the daylight hours. I am certain we will devise a plan."

"No camp today," Hundred said. "As exposed as that makes us, standing still for too long would be worse. I have faith that snow and fog will obscure us from above.

If we make good time, we will be at the gates around nightfall."

"And then we will see," said Egda. "That is, you will see, and I will listen. If we encounter anyone on the road, remember our aliases: Engelbert, Hilda, Otto, and Ethel. Swords, stay hidden, ready if needed. Great peril lies at Kyles Frost, but there is danger enough on the approach for all of us."

They were back on the road in moments, having never truly unpacked in the first place. The snow had eased off, but thick mist clung to the steep cliffs like white veils to a tearful cheek. Shapes loomed out of the mist as they rounded each tight bend — rocks, every time, but making Eleanor's heart race all the same. She expected discovery and threat at any moment. The only thing that worried her more was the steep drop-off where the road met the open air. One missed step in the flowing fog could be her last . . .

An hour into their ascent, Egda surprised them all by starting to sing. In a clear if slightly cracked voice that vanished into the muffling fog, he began the first line of "Fools and Kings" and sang it all the way through to the end.

"What's he doing?" Eleanor hissed. "If people can't see us, they'll hear us for sure."

"I believe that's the plan," said Hundred. "If you were looking for someone traveling in secret, and you heard this racket, would you ever suspect?"

"They might shoot us just to shut us up." But Eleanor grinned and joined in on "Green Leaves," followed by "The Soldier's Song" and "Meat, Mead, and Mother." Where she forgot the words, she simply sang the notes. Odo knew them all — one of the dubious benefits of belonging to a big family that enjoyed regular sing-alongs — and he had a sweet, light voice that belied his size. Had he been higher-born and not found a sword while looking for eels in a dying river, Eleanor reflected, he might have become a troubadour.

At that moment, both of them were happy that he hadn't. There was something about singing in the face of danger that swept away all concerns, apart from keeping to the path and holding the pitch. Everything else could wait . . . except when it couldn't.

Twice they encountered parties going back the other way, both on foot. Odo and Eleanor kept their hands near their hidden swords in case they posed a threat.

The travelers all warned them of the blocked pass ahead and advised them to turn back.

"More snow coming," said one, a barrel-maker with bright red cheeks, possibly from drinking too much of the wine his wares contained. "And no sign of relenting among the ironheads at the gate. Never seen such stubbornness in all my days. You'd think an army of rebels was on its way to storm the gates of Winterset itself!"

"Is that what they're saying?" asked Hundred with carefully manufactured alarm. "An army? We don't want to get caught in a fight."

"They're not saying anything, no matter who asks.

One of those newfangled 'Instruments' is up there. Called Colvert. She's been there three months, acting as afraid as a lamb in a wolf den. I hear there's an Adjustor up there as well, sticking their nose into everything, although why one of them would bother with Kyles Frost is beyond my ken. It's just a road with a door. Everything worked better when Sir Jolan was in charge . . . ah, that is to say, I thought it might . . . ah . . . forget what I've said, would you?"

Hundred thanked him for the warning, but said that she and her wit-addled father and ingrate grandchildren would try their luck all the same. They couldn't keep the pass closed forever, could they?

On his well-meant warning being ignored, the barrel-maker and his entourage went on their way with a shrug. As they rounded the next bend, the singing that had caught their ears resumed as carefree as before. They'd soon learn, the barrel-maker thought.

None in the traveling choir was as carefree as they sounded. *An Adjustor*, the barrel-maker had said. They'd had trouble enough with Instruments, and only escaped one of them by extremely good fortune. What new troubles — and additional forces — might this higher official bring?

It was a fear they didn't voice aloud, in case less friendly ears were listening.

After a long rendition of the round-song "My Merry Lad," Odo declared his voice too hoarse to go on. Hundred agreed, saying that the pass was close anyway, so perhaps observant silence was preferable. Tip unfolded his delicate ears and went gratefully to sleep.

Before they had gone much farther, Eleanor became aware of a rising rumble from ahead, with a strange hissing laid over the top of it. It reminded her of the sound of the Silverrun in full flood, but oddly different.

"What's that noise?" she asked.

"The Foss," said Hundred. "It is a waterfall that plunges one thousand feet from the lake that fills the pass and becomes the Suthgemare River, which wends all the way to the Southern Ocean. Our road leads over it."

"Won't we get wet?" asked Odo.

"No."

"That's a relief," said Eleanor with a shiver. "And what about the lake? Is there a bridge?"

"One challenge at a time. To gain the lake, we must first pass through the gate."

Eleanor and Odo returned to fretting. Surely there was no possibility of passing undiscovered. One glance at Egda's nose and eyes would reveal his identity. All the guards had to do was pull back his hood and everything would be lost.

"You must have come through here plenty of times," said Eleanor to Runnel. "How would you do it?"

"𝔐y knights have always been in the service of their king and therefore had permission to pass," the sword said. "Under present circumstances, one knight alone might bypass the guards in stealth, but not four, with horses."

Odo was having a similar conversation with Biter. "If a frontal assault is out, a diversion is too dangerous, we can't sneak past, and we don't have very good disguises, I just don't see how we can possibly get through."

"𝔚e can only trust that our liege has a plan that doesn't

involve leading us to certain death," the sword advised him. "In that unlikely event, though . . . promise me that I won't end up in the water. I could not bear to sleep with the eels again. I would rather be melted down for a cart brace than lose still more of my memories."

With Hundred unwilling to reveal her thoughts, all they could do was fidget and wait.

TWELVE

The road led between walls of sheer stone that blotted out the sun. To their left, a steep drop plummeted into darkness, from which emerged the sound of churning water. As the road became narrower, the thunder of the Foss grew louder until it filled their senses. Finally, the waterfall itself appeared, revealed as the cliff walls parted in sweeping curves to form a giant bowl ringed with craggy, snow-topped peaks, the two largest, Twisletoth and Tindit, vanishing into a dense roof of clouds.

Ahead, the road crossed a natural rock bridge spanning from one side of the pass to the other. Out of a ragged hole under this bridge spewed forth a torrent of water wider and more violent than any Odo or Eleanor had ever imagined. Foam sprayed in white flecks and became a mist that painted their faces in chilling damp. With a roar that rocked them to the bones, the torrent vanished into the chasm below, beginning its journey to the far-off sea.

Wordlessly — for what was the point in even trying to talk? — Hundred waved them forward, onto the bridge. The stone was slick and slippery, the violence of the water so great Odo feared the bridge might shatter under them at any moment.

But Hundred did not hesitate, so he followed resolutely, looking neither to the left nor the right, concentrating only on Wiggy's footing.

When he reached the other side, he felt as though his bones had turned to jelly. He reached down to pat Wiggy on the flank, grateful for the mare's steady footing and nerves.

Egda came next, then Eleanor, looking as shocked as she felt. Only when she was safely on the other side did she stick her tongue out to taste the spray. It was cold and clean — pure water from glaciers higher up the mountains. It made her feel very much alive, and grateful to be so.

Hundred led them on, through a dense cloud that covered the road, hiding what lay ahead. When they passed safely through it, their challenge was laid bare before them: another rock bridge much larger than the first, topped with a heavy wooden wall with gates midway, leading farther into the hills. The gate looked impregnable, studded with iron bolts and braced in holes dug deep into the rock. Below, where the road joined the bridge, several wagons clustered, covered and uncovered, waiting to proceed. Some had pitched tents and lit fires. Odo's stomach rumbled at the thought of hot food. Or was that nerves? It was hard to tell.

A dozen armed guards stood in front of the gates. Eleanor's sharp eyes picked out the gleam of helmets on ledges high above, undoubtedly the archers that Tip had described.

On a narrow balustrade above the gates stood a tall figure dressed entirely in red. Eleanor couldn't see this person's eyes, but it was clear they watched the road and all who proceeded along it. Fortunately, snow still fell, obscuring them from close scrutiny. The sun had long disappeared behind the mountaintops and would within half an hour set completely.

Instead of leading them directly to the gate, Hundred turned to join the wagons.

"The chill sits heavily in my bones," she called back to them, adopting her "Hilda" voice. "Let's rest here awhile and see what causes the delay. At the very least we can avail ourselves of a fire, if these good people will make space for us."

Her cry was heard over the roaring of the Foss. Two young lads scampered from the wagons to help with their horses in exchange for a copper farthing each, and soon they were gathered around a campfire, warming their hands and hearing the story about the Adjustor's blocking of the pass once more.

"Aye, madness, it is indeed," agreed a carpenter clad from head to waist in what looked like one thick brown scarf, wrapped many times around him. His hands stayed hidden, held close to his body for warmth. All they could clearly see of his face was his mouth. "I have a shipment of doors due in Wohness tomorrow morning and I won't be paid if they don't arrive on time."

"And I've a herd of goats that won't survive another night without forage," grumbled another traveler. She passed around a flask of warming spirits that made Odo's eyes water, just sniffing at it. "We're going to lose our livelihoods, and who will help us? Not those wretched Instruments, and not that Adjustor neither. They only care about making us follow the rules — rules that make about as much sense as a partridge in a pie shop!"

The grumbling became a steady rumble from the dozen or so people gathered around the fire. Odo and Eleanor had been enlisted into a game of knucklebones played by the other children gathered there. Odo deliberately lost and was cast out of the ongoing competition, so he could pay attention to what the adults were saying. Eleanor was more competitive and rose steadily through the ranks, beating one after another of the local champions.

"Has anyone ever considered standing up to them?" asked Hundred, speaking in a low voice in case any guards were in earshot.

"What can we do?" asked the goat herder. "We're just honest folk trying to turn one penny into two. The prince tells the Regulators what to do, they tell the Adjustors, the Adjustors tell the Instruments, and the Instruments and their guards do what they will."

"I hear it's not the prince at all," said the carpenter very softly. "It's the regent who's brought in all the new non-sense and sent away the knights. All these money-grubbing new officials answer to *her*."

"That sounds like dangerous talk to me," said "Hilda" as her ancient, hooded father poked at the end of a pro-truding stump with a booted foot, making sparks fly up from the fire. "If word were to reach the Adjustor of what you were saying —"

The carpenter's eyes narrowed and his hand closed on a chisel in the box at his side.

"I've already lost everything," he said grimly. "Or at least I will have if those doors don't arrive tomorrow. And I doubt anyone here will betray me to the guards. They'd better not try, anyway."

"Peace! Your loss is my loss, friend." Hundred leaned closer and spoke so softly that Odo could only make out a fragment of what she said. "Perhaps . . . you and I . . . solution to both our problems . . ."

The carpenter sized her up with a long look, then nodded. Together, they moved out of the firelight to talk in private.

Odo watched them go, wondering what she was up to.

"Yes!" Eleanor clapped her hands in triumph, then reached out to shake hands with her fallen opponent, a boy her age who accepted defeat with a surly grimace. "Shall we play again?"

A chorus of disillusioned nays was the reply, and gradually the other children wandered off, leaving Odo and Eleanor alone.

"If you'll keep an eye on, uh, Grandfather here," he said, "I'll go check on the horses."

"Right you are, Otto. I'm happy to stay here in the warm."

Odo walked off through the ring of wagons to where the ten horses were hobbled in two close lines, each mount under a warm blanket. They whinnied and shifted restlessly as Odo approached, their hooves crunching and squeaking on the snow. The night was bright from the moon and stars, but very cold, Odo's breath billowing out in soft white clouds. There was no sign of Hundred. Whatever she was doing, she had to do it soon if they were to pass Kyles Frost in time to save the prince.

He raised both hands, as though warming his fingers on his breath, and spoke softly through them.

"All quiet out here?"

"Nothing to report, Sir Odo," said Biter from his hiding place.

"If anyone comes too close," said Runnel, "we'll do our best talking-horse impersonation to scare them off."

"You'll do no such thing!" snapped Biter. "A talking horse is hardly less conspicuous than a talking sword —"

"Obviously. Let me have my joke. It is boring out here with no one but you and the horses to listen to. They are pleasant creatures, but one can only bear so much on the subjects of oats and eels."

With a flutter of wings, Tip dropped out of the sky and clung to Wiggy's bridle. Half a moth protruded from his mouth.

"Any movement around the gates?" Odo asked him.

Tip gulped down the moth. "n! o!"

"Do you know where Hundred is?"

"b! e! h! i! n! d! y! o! u!"

Odo turned and there she was, coming out from between two of the wagons and walking toward him.

"We need to shed six horses," she told him in a low voice. "I'll leave you to choose. Have the remaining four ready to leave as quickly as possible, but do so without making it look obvious. Wait for me here."

"We won't be able to carry all our supplies."

"We don't need them. Where's your sister, Ethel?"

"By the fire, with, uh, Engelbert."

"Good. I have a job for her too."

With that, Hundred vanished back into the dark, as though she had never been there.

Eleanor was playing with Egda and marveling at how he could catch the knucklebones he couldn't see when Hundred suddenly appeared next to her.

"Father," she said to Egda. "You're looking unwell. This cold is not good for you. Our new friend Wilheard has generously offered us shelter in his wagon. This way."

She lifted Egda by one elbow and Eleanor took the other. He played the weak, old man with aplomb, shuffling listlessly away from the fire. Those remaining in the warmth offered their sympathy while at the same time wishing that they too had the opportunity to find protection from the freezing night.

"Wilheard is the carpenter," Hundred whispered to Eleanor and Egda. "His caravan is the covered blue one — you can see the pile of doors poking out the back. Knock twice and do as he says. I will meet you there in a moment."

She disappeared again, leaving the two of them to wind their way through the wagons and horses forming the temporary camp.

"What's she up to?" Eleanor wondered aloud.

Egda tapped the side of his nose, but said nothing.

*　*　*

Odo had just finished choosing the horses and reorganizing the supplies when Hundred returned. He had picked Wiggy among the four. With Tip securely hanging from her bridle, he turned at the sound of footsteps.

"Bring them all," Hundred said, taking the reins of her preferred horse and leading him after her. The rest trailed obediently along, Odo and Wiggy alert for stragglers. They came around the camp to a long wagon with a blue canopy covering the front third and a high load of rectangular doors securely roped into the back two-thirds. Four worn but worthy nags were hitched to the back of the wagon. Hundred rapped twice on the side.

The carpenter opened a flap in the canvas. Past him, Odo could see Eleanor and Egda sitting at a narrow table, still warmly dressed despite the heat of the small traveling stove next to them.

"We're ready," said the carpenter from within his thick, looping scarf.

Odo blinked. It wasn't the carpenter's voice. It was Egda's — and the person sitting at the table wearing Egda's hood wasn't Egda at all, but a man similar in size whose face Odo had never seen before. The girl wasn't Eleanor, either, but a woman in Odo's spare woolen hat. They had switched places!

The real Eleanor peered out past Egda. She was wearing different outer clothes too, most notably a huge, brightly colored scarf wrapped many times around her neck and over most of her face.

"I'm much warmer now," she said with a grin. "Got the horses?"

Hundred nudged Odo inside and shut the flap behind her.

"Six horses, as per the arrangement," she told Wilheard. "Fair trade for the wagon and your clothes. We will do our best to deliver the doors, or see that you are paid for them in full at a later date. If you go back to Ablerhyll, we will send word to you there."

"If not," the carpenter said, "the horses will fetch a good price. They are fine beasts."

He spat in his palm and held it out to Hundred. They shook.

"Don't forget to carry on the act until the morning," Eleanor said. "Offer to play knucklebones with the other kids. That'll scare them off."

The carpenter and his wife left the wagon, doing a passable impression of an ancient old man and his great-granddaughter. It was just possible, Eleanor thought, that this plan could work.

"What about me and Hundred?" Odo asked. "There's no disguise for us."

"You and your grandmother have to get through in search of mountain wort to cure her joint fever, and we're simply helping you along."

"But why would they let a granny and her grandson through when they won't let anyone else?"

"Because the grandmother will have something that will convince them to do so."

"What?" asked Odo.

"Leave that to me," said Hundred. "I heard something

promising from the others who've tried to get past, and I can be very persuasive when I have to be."

Egda chuckled. "Wasn't that what you told Headstrong Harold at the siege of Dysig?"

"It was indeed," she said. "That's how he got his new nickname, Headless Harold."

THIRTEEN

Eleanor didn't feel nervous until the wagon started moving, drawn by their four remaining horses up the road toward the gate. She sat inside with Hundred, peering out through a hole in the canvas while Odo drove, Egda sitting comfortably at his side, disguised as the carpenter. Both swords were hidden again, this time in a long storage space under a seat, Biter grumbling about being constantly kept in the dark.

"Fear not, little brother," Runnel reassured him. "If this plan goes awry, you will have your time in the light."

The gate was brightly lit by many torches set in iron stands along the road, as well as two big lanterns above the gate. The guards must have heard the wagon before they saw it, because half a dozen had already turned out, archers with arrows notched.

The wagon trundled onto the rock bridge and stopped as one of the guards held up her hand. Tip circled overhead, invisible in the gloom.

"Go back!" yelled the guard. "Go to sleep!"

"We've got papers now!" Egda shouted back in a surprisingly good imitation of the carpenter's voice.

The guard looked over her shoulder. A moment later, an officious-looking woman in the red-and-silver uniform of an Instrument, with a huge bearskin cloak thrown over it, emerged from a sally port in the main gate. She stalked over to the wagon, chin up and nose wrinkled as if facing something highly unpleasant and much beneath her.

"You again, Wilheard? I've already told you you're not going through."

"I beg your pardon, Instrument Colvert," Egda said, keeping his head down as if being extra humble but really to keep his face hidden under his hood, deep in the shade of the canopy. "The thing is, this young lad and his grandmother have special dispensation from the regent to pass through, and I've volunteered to drive them."

"Dispensation? What are they, spies?"

"Not our business to know. I suppose the regent has her reasons too."

"And I suppose you thought you could deliver your beloved doors into the bargain, I bet."

"Ain't no harm in turning a good turn into a profit, is there?"

"I suppose not."

Instrument Colvert chewed the inside of her lip uneasily. Odo tried to look superior and threatening in a non-knightly way. He had never met a spy before, but supposed they looked much like ordinary people, or else they wouldn't be much use as spies at all.

"Dispensation, eh? Well, I guess they've got a letter to prove it. With the proper seal. Let's see it."

Egda fished under his winding scarf. "I've got it here. Seems in order to me, but you'd know better than a humble tradesman."

A leather scroll case passed from Egda's hands to the Instrument's. She opened one end and tipped it up. Blank parchment slid into her waiting palm — and so did six gold nobles.

She looked at the coins, eyes widening in surprise, then up at Egda and Odo.

Odo held his breath. A bribe! A massive bribe. Six gold nobles was more than a simple carpenter could make in a year, maybe two! But this was where everything could go entirely wrong. If Instrument Colvert's loyalty to the regent was fierce enough, she could expose them with a word, and then the arrows would fly.

Her eyes gleamed as brightly as the coins, then narrowed in speculation.

"Do you feel that chill?" said Egda with a shiver. "Must be hard up here, night after night, listening to the likes of me complaining. At least we can turn around and go home whenever we want. How long since your family saw you last, eh? A week? A month? Longer? If only you could offer them comfort until you return . . ."

Instrument Colvert's hand closed over the coins and slipped them into her pocket.

"These look in order to me," she said, replacing the paper and the lid of the scroll case and handing it back to Egda. "I will order the gates opened."

"And our friend the Adjustor?"

"The Adjustor is asleep. I'll let him know in the morning. Who are we to interfere with the regent's business?"

With that she turned and reentered through the postern door. A moment later, with a great clunking and groaning, the gates swung out, revealing the road beyond.

Odo kept his face carefully neutral, praying his relief was perfectly concealed. So far, so good, but there was a way yet to go.

Inside the wagon, Eleanor, who had followed the conversation but not seen the coins, marveled at the ruse.

"How — ?"

Hundred explained. "I had heard this Instrument was open to bribes, but the others waiting simply couldn't offer enough. These Instruments are lackeys brazenly seeking advantage in a new regime; greed is the one thing they all share. Let us hope that the Adjustor is no less greedy, and they share the bribe and keep their mouths shut."

The wagon rocked over uneven flagstones through the gateway. It was more than twenty paces deep, with a portcullis at the far side that was raised by the time they reached it. Odo flicked the reins, willing himself not to look back, and urged the horses out into the open air.

The moon had risen higher and now lit up the land ahead, including the teardrop-shaped lake Hundred had described to them. It was as large as Lenburh, a tarn fed by glacial meltwater from the surrounding mountains. This, then, was the source of the Foss, the waterfall he could still feel rumbling underfoot. And yet, as he approached the lake, following the snow-covered track that led down the rock bridge to the nearest shore, he could see that it was frozen. Obviously, the ice didn't penetrate entirely down to its depths, otherwise there would be no water to flow anywhere.

"Keep going," said Egda, "onto the ice. It is very thick, and will carry us. Aim for that spur of rock on the far side, the one that looks like a flag. It marks the road down."

"Is there another gate to get through?" Odo asked.

"No, but there will be a small garrison stationed on the other side. They do not normally stir, as the gate is the main defense. With luck they will pay us little heed."

Odo urged the horses warily onto the ice. It held, as promised. Many other wagons had come this way, and their iron-shod wheels had scored a rough road across the surface. Even so, horses and wheels slipped from time to time, and they could only move slowly across the ice. Tip swooped down to fly alongside them, wings flapping hard.

Eleanor came out of the canopied cabin and sat next to Odo on the driver's bench. With a whoop of delight, she marveled at them heading across a lake of ice in the middle of the mountains, under the moon! She couldn't wait to tell her father when they got home.

"We made it!" she cried. "I thought we were going to have to fight our way through for sure."

"Do not tempt fate," cautioned Hundred, sticking her head out between them to look ahead. "We are not safe yet."

"What can they do now?"

Odo told her about the garrison on the other side of the lake.

"Just remember that you are supposed to be Wigburg," said Hundred. "She has likely been this way many times and is no longer prone to whooping."

"How could anyone ever get tired of this view?" Eleanor craned her neck to take in the complete moonlit vista. Looking behind them, she asked, "Do they always let off fireworks when people come through the gate?"

Odo risked a glance over his shoulder. A bright red light was shooting up into the sky, dripping fiery sparks and casting a bloody pall across the snow.

"No!" exclaimed Hundred. "That is a flare alerting the garrison ahead that we are to be stopped. The Instrument has betrayed us!"

Odo instinctively flicked the reins to drive the horses faster, but Hundred reached out and made him loosen them again.

"We cannot risk speed," she said. "If a horse falls or we overturn, then all is lost. Keep up the pace."

They were perhaps halfway across the lake.

"Who gave us away?" fumed Eleanor. "It couldn't have been Wilheard or Wigburg, could it? And the Adjustor took your money!"

"Unfortunately, those who can be bought do not always stay that way. I think this proves that the Adjustors are more afraid of their superiors — and the regent — than we expected."

Odo concentrated on the horses. The pretense was done. All that mattered now was escape. Eleanor called for the swords, and they instantly appeared, Runnel joining her knight as she clambered up onto the top of the load of doors at the rear of the wagon, following Hundred, and Biter floating in the air next to Odo like a giant dart. Egda remained with Odo on the driver's bench, staff at the ready.

"Hurry the horses as we leave the ice and pass the garrison fort," Hundred told Odo. "Trust in speed to throw off the aim of the archers and the horses' hooves to deter any guards who try to bar our passage."

At speed, the gate was barely a minute away. Already he could see the wooden palisade of the guardhouse, torches flaring and metal helmets shining as guards raced to get onto the walls.

Suddenly, Tip was flying next to him, chittering urgently.

"What's that you're saying?" he asked.

"l! o! o! k! l! e! f! t!"

He glanced in that direction and saw a large shape loping across the ice. It was a bear, such a dark brown it looked almost black in the night, and it was running right for them.

"a! n! d! r! i! g! h! t!"

Two more shapes, larger even than the bear and with long, lethally sharp-looking horns and teeth. Also running.

"Gore yaks!" cried Hundred. "It seems we have craft-fire to contend with too."

"Look," said Eleanor, pointing in the rough direction of Twisletoth, on whose flanks a green spark flickered, sign of a craft-fire. "That flare wasn't just to alert the guards ahead."

"Would that we were up there rather than here," Hundred growled. "Then we would see a match! How do we go, Sir Odo? Will we outrace these creatures before reaching our human enemies?"

"I . . . I don't think so," he gasped, panting with the effort of controlling the horses. They could smell the bear and were anxious to flee from it. Both the bear and the gore yaks were running along such a path as to cut them off some distance from the top of the road, where the guards awaited them. "They're going to get to us first."

"You and I will take the bear, Sir Odo," said Biter. "It will be no match for our combined strength."

"And we are no match for the rain of arrows that will inevitably fall on us if we stop," said Hundred grimly.

"Our options are sorely limited," Egda declared. "There is, however, one we have not discussed. A more direct route to the bottom than any winding road."

"The Ghyll?" Hundred's expression turned to alarm. "Sire, that would be madness."

"Where madness blinds, inspiration may find." The old man gripped his friend's shoulder. "It is our only chance."

"Who or what's the Ghyll?" Eleanor asked, made extremely nervous by Hundred's reaction.

"It lies through that notch yonder," said Hundred, pointing at a triangle segment cut of the surrounding mountainsides, not far from where the guards waited. "Once, there were two waterfalls leading from this lake to the plains below. One was the Foss, which you have already seen. The other, by far the more dangerous, was the Ghyll."

"We can't swim down a waterfall!" exclaimed Odo, thinking of the horses as well as themselves.

"That would indeed be impossible," Egda said, "if the Ghyll had not frozen solid, long ago. And it is not a single vertical fall, but a series of many low falls."

Eleanor gaped at him, remembering her desire to skate down a glacier. "My father always says, 'Be careful what you wish for.' Now I know why!"

"It is madness," Hundred said again. "We will never survive."

"We can go around the yaks at the last minute," said Odo, calculating distances and times. "We'll surprise them."

"That is only the first of our trials. The ice will smash us to pieces!"

"Not if we ride the doors!" exclaimed Eleanor. "Wilheard's doors! We can use them as sleds. If we hang on tight and brake where we can —"

"Madness," said Hundred for the third time, but her teeth were bared now. It was almost a smile. "Move quickly! We have mere moments to prepare."

She looked after Egda while Eleanor prepared for Odo. His armor and pack were heavy, and so was the door she unshipped for him from the stack, but weight was no concern. She didn't even notice it. Her heart was pounding, and the night seemed alight. Urgency kept her thoughts off what a frozen waterfall might look like, one even more violent than the Foss.

When she looked up with a cry of "Ready!" she saw that the bear and gore yaks and guards were now frighteningly close. The animals' eyes were smoke-filled from the sorcery of the craft-fire. Archers drew back their bows.

Odo wrenched the reins hard to his right, and the horses reared up in protest, throwing slivers of ice from their hooves. Then they found their purpose again, along with their purchase, and began to gallop for their lives. The wagon bounced and lurched, almost overturning, newly loosened doors falling off the back. Everyone held on for grim life, Odo cursing as he now tried to hold the terrified horses back.

The wagon lurched onto two wheels, nearly tipped, then steadied on a new course, heading past the snarling yaks and directly for the top of the Ghyll. Arrows flew, but all fell short or were chopped out of the air by Eleanor and Hundred. Two struck the beasts, who howled in rage as they skidded on the ice to follow their quarry.

"Steady!" urged Egda, crouching besides Odo and pointing his staff forward as though he could see the way ahead. "Steady!"

Shouts went up from the guards. A score or more emerged from the guardhouse waving swords and pikes, their spiked boots giving them ample purchase on the ice. If the Ghyll proved unpassable for any reason, Eleanor thought, they would have to fight humans as well as beasts in order to survive.

Her heart was in her throat as they reached the notch.

Odo put every tiny scrap of strength he possessed into hauling back on the reins, as Hundred slammed on the brake. The horses saw the drop too and turned violently, breaking their traces and running free. The wagon sped on, teetering on two wheels, bouncing and skidding as everyone on board screamed or shouted, including the swords, before finally hitting a ridge of ice and slowly toppling over.

"Move!" cried Hundred, tossing the door she would share with Egda from the top of the wagon. Eleanor obeyed, with packs and armor to follow. She ignored the roaring of the beasts and the shouting of the soldiers. She put everything out of her mind except for the plan, their one and only chance of survival, quickly lashing her pack to the door and testing the looped handholds she had made for herself and Odo.

But when she glanced down the Ghyll, she faltered.

A narrow, jagged ravine led down the side of the mountain. Sandwiched between those lethal stone walls was a dragon's tongue of pure white, curving and twisting into savage bends and turns, surrounded on every side by knife-sharp edges and bone-smashing boulders, any one of which might kill her.

Odo joined her to carry the door to the very edge of the frozen waterfall. The first part of it was an almost vertical drop of a dozen paces or more, before it leveled out for a while and then went into a series of frighteningly steep curves.

But the bear and the gore yaks were almost upon them. There was no time to waste.

"Care to join me, Sir Eleanor?"

"I believe I will, Sir Odo."

The two knights lay full-length on their door, swords hovering overhead, and gripped the rope handles.

"Three, two, one — go!" they cried together.

They pushed off, Hundred and Egda hot on their heels. Then all was ice and speed and falling — and screaming, definitely screaming — as they raced for death or the bottom of the Ghyll, whichever came first.

FOURTEEN

Prince Kendryk hardly ever slept these days. Finishing the mural, and finishing it quickly, was all that mattered. He could tell from the gloating in his grandmother's voice that time was running out.

When he did sleep, he dreamed of the earth shaking and splitting open, and huge gouts of flame blazing forth, as though the very world was ending.

He was in the middle of one of these dreams when a rough hand shook him awake. He was confused for a long moment. Was the ground shaking, or was he? Had he finished the mural at last and brought his plan to completion, or was it all unfinished and the outcome still unknown? Sometimes he wished he could simply let it go, and maybe if the outcome for Tofte wouldn't be so awful, he would have. Personal gain wasn't what he craved, and never had been.

"Look at him, sleeping on the floor like some common drab," the regent muttered. "Wake up, Grandson! I have better things to do than attend to madmen in belfries."

Kendryk sat up, rubbing his eyes. The person shaking him was Lord Deor, the Chief Regulator. Kendryk flinched away from his rough touch, and Lord Deor stepped back, executing the merest sketch of a bow as he went. The scabbard of his heavy sword dragged along the ground with a harsh scraping sound.

"He is awake, Your Highness."

"About time." She took Lord Deor's place at Kendryk's feet, not deigning to stoop. She towered over him like the throne she coveted, a tall structure of wood and gold that made anyone sitting in it look simultaneously very small and extremely self-important.

"I have news of your great-uncle," she said without preamble. "The *former* king. You must brace yourself."

Kendryk placed his outspread hands on the stone floor. "I am as braced as I will ever be, Grandmother."

"He is dead," she said. "I received word this morning. There can be no doubt."

The news, though half expected, was still shocking. Kendryk's eyes flooded with tears, and he sensed the world crowding in around him like the walls of a prison. Was he truly alone now? Did he have no one to turn to but himself?

Dragon, dragon, heed our call . . .

He looked up, past his grandmother, to the mural. It was so nearly finished. He had hoped for more time, but now, perhaps, there was none.

"I see that you are as shocked as I was," Odelyn said without any trace of shock at all. Egda's sister, the regent, the architect of everything that had befallen Tofte in recent months, had no lost love for her brother. "Knowing that it would be your wish, I have declared a state funeral for three days from now. The kingdom will pause in his honor and bid a final farewell to a great king."

The slight emphasis on *great* was all for Kendryk.

"Yes," he said through his grief. "That is a good decision."

"I thought you would be pleased, although . . ." She took three steps in a half circle, coming around so he sat between her and a wide-smiling Lord Deor. ". . . I do hate to tread on my brother's memory. My coronation is of course scheduled for *two* days from now. I considered a delay, but why, when the nation is in need of succor? What better time for a new beginning?"

Coldness spread from Kendryk's heart through the rest of his body.

"You think you have won."

"I have, Grandson. Did you really think you would ever wear the crown? You are not fit to be king, and you know it."

There's only one way to find out, he thought but did not say.

"I will accept your congratulations at a later date," she said. "You are grief-stricken at the news of your great-uncle's fate. We must remember that the last Old Dragon lived longer than anyone expected, and console ourselves with the knowledge that the kingdom will be well cared for in his wake."

Kendryk could take no more of her gloating. He had but one question for her, and then she could be gone.

"Will there be a viewing?" he asked.

Her lips tightened under that proud, jutting nose.

"Why do you ask?"

"I wish to pay my respects."

"There will be a coffin, but no viewing. The body is too . . . damaged."

"You have seen it with your own eyes?"

"I have not," she admitted, "but there can be no doubt. No doubt at all. I have it on the word of no less than three Instruments and one Adjustor. The old man is dead at long last . . . so thoroughly dead that not even his most loyal supporter could doubt it."

He had heard her slight hesitation, and wondered at it.

"How can anyone be more thoroughly dead than just . . . dead?" he asked.

Lord Deor's smile slipped off his face like blood off a burnished shield.

"There has been an abundance of royal deaths," the regent said. "I am informed that Egda died defending a nowhere place called Lenburh in the jaws of a bilewolf. I am also informed that he died in a town called Ablerhyll after a terrible accident. I am further informed that he died at Kyles Frost while foolishly attempting to sled down the Ghyll. He can't have died in all three places — but he is sure to have died in one of them. Lord Deor is looking into it. I expect he'll have it resolved before the memorial. Won't you, Lord Deor?"

The Chief Regulator bowed, shooting Kendryk a murderous look. His right hand never strayed from the hilt of his sword.

"We will leave you to your grief, Grandson," the regent told him. "Rest assured that your troubles will soon be over. The crown that would sit so heavily on your tortured brow will soon sit on mine, and you may spend all your days daubing paint on walls, knowing the kingdom is well cared for. Who would not be satisfied with such an arrangement?"

She gestured dismissively at the mural, its sweeping lines and jagged points, and he was left with no illusions as to his fate. Yes, he might live beyond the coronation itself, but how long until he was found at the foot of a ladder with his neck broken? Or subtly poisoned by something slipped into one of his paints?

Not that there would be any point painting once Odelyn was crowned king of Tofte. If he didn't finish the mural before then, all his efforts would have been for naught.

The regent and the Chief Regulator swept out of the tower room without so much as a glance behind them. They saw no threat in him, and that was exactly as it should be.

Two days. Time hadn't quite run out yet. There was still a chance.

Looking up into the shadows high above, he sought the black, flitting shapes he knew would be there. One, the smallest, swooped down to catch his outstretched arm.

"Do you have a message, Tip?" he whispered.

The tiny bat shook his head and looked up at him with sorrowful eyes.

"All right, then, little friend. You'd better tell me what happened."

FIFTEEN

The last thing Eleanor remembered was the sound of ice crunching against wood and being battered back and forth like a ball in a barrel, with Odo at her side and Runnel and Biter swooping in to try to lever their makeshift sled away from the most obvious dangers of the icy slope. That memory of the terrifying ice slide seemed to stretch on and on, but finally there had been an obstacle that could not be dodged, a sudden flight into the air, Odo shouting, the swords screaming — and then a blow to her head that flung her into darkness. It echoed as though it meant to go on forever.

Waking was much worse.

Eleanor sat upright and clutched desperately at her face. Something — a furred hand? — was pressed tightly over her mouth and nose. She was suffocating!

Her fingers found purchase, pulled, and suddenly light and air returned. For a moment, all she could do was gasp in breaths. She barely saw the dappled light of the clearing in which she found herself, or the splintered ruin of the doors that lay around her, or the tumbled disorder of packs and armor.

The first thing she truly noted was Odo, who lay struggling on his back next to her. There was a giant moth over his face. It was as large as a dinner plate, a match for the one that had been attached to her.

"Ugh!"

Fighting dizziness, she crouched over him and tore at the creature with both hands. It was surprisingly strong, with long legs that hung on tightly to his ears and hair, and curling antennae that batted at her eyes. Finally, she ripped it away, and it fluttered angrily off into the trees.

"What was that thing?" Odo wheezed in revulsion, catching his breath. He looked around. "Where are we?"

"Giant moth," she said. "And I have no idea."

But they were alive — and the immediate priority was finding Egda and Hundred. Eleanor staggered uneasily to her feet, red blotches still dotting her vision. There! Another ruined door, and Hundred grappling with her own smothering moth. Nearby lay Egda, his gold blindfold off and face tightly wrapped up in gray-and-brown wings. He wasn't moving.

"Gah!" Hundred freed herself the moment Eleanor reached their liege. They took one wing each and pulled with all their might. The moth tore in half and came away with a ghastly ripping sound. Egda fell back on the mossy ground, eyes half open, insensible even to Hundred's firm slap across his cheeks.

"He can't be dead," Odo said. "He can't be!"

"He isn't," said Hundred, resting her head against the old man's chest. "But his heart is slowing down. We must restore its rhythm — somehow."

"I saw my father do this once." Eleanor frantically cast her mind back, clutching at details that eluded her. "Old Osgar . . . at the fair . . . one punch to the chest . . ."

"A slap to the sternum might well do it," said Hundred, beginning to look frantic as the seconds passed and still Egda did not stir. "With the heel of the hand, if it were powerful enough. But it could also kill —"

"We have to try," whispered Eleanor.

They all looked at each other. No one wanted to be the one who killed the king, even if it was in an attempt to save him.

"Let me through," said Odo after what seemed like minutes, but was only seconds. He bent down, raised his right hand, and brought it down hard where Eleanor indicated.

Egda flopped like an eel, coughed three times, and opened his sightless eyes.

"My liege," said Hundred, her voice betraying such relief that Eleanor had never imagined she could possess.

"I dreamed," he said in a ragged voice, "of sliding down the refuse chute at Winterset . . . and landing in a mountain of old pillows . . . feathers rose up to choke me . . ."

With uncanny accuracy, he reached out to clutch Hundred's wrist.

"We survived!"

"Indeed," she said, patting the hand gripping her. "We would not have, but for the quick thinking of these two young knights."

Eleanor caught Odo's eye. *Knights*, not *knightlings*.

"But are we safe?" Egda went on. "Were we followed? We must move quickly, ere we are discovered —"

"We will, my liege. First, we must ascertain where we are. A forest of some kind . . . probably the upper reaches of the Groanwood. There were smother-moths."

Egda rubbed his throat and sat up. "The work of our enemy?"

"Most likely happenstance, or else worse would have come by now."

"It may yet be on its way."

Odo looked around him, at the close-packed trunks and the shadows beyond. There could be anything out there.

Feeling suddenly vulnerable, he reached for Biter but found his scabbard empty. So was Eleanor's.

"The swords," he said. "Biter and Runnel — where are they?"

Hundred checked her side. The curved blade that usually hung there was present.

"Inspect the wreckage!"

The three of them scrambled through the broken doors, but found nothing but Egda's staff.

"This is most mysterious," said Hundred.

"They wouldn't just leave," said Eleanor. "Would they?"

A twig crunched in the undergrowth. They spun to face it. Odo reached down to pick up a branch and hefted it in one hand, wishing he was at least wearing his armor. Eleanor did the same.

"Who's there?" she called. "Come out where we can see you!"

An enormous hooded figure parted the bracken — a man easily a foot taller than Odo. He raised his hands to tug back the hood, revealing a scalp that was utterly bare of hair; deep, hooded eyes; and a face pockmarked with scars, like burns made by fiery sparks.

Craft-fire, thought Eleanor in alarm. Perhaps the moths hadn't been natural after all.

"To me!" cried Hundred, and Eleanor and Odo moved at the same instant, putting themselves in front of Egda. Without swords, without even knives, they would defend their liege to the death.

As the giant moved toward them, two familiar voices cried out from the bracken.

"Sir Odo!"

"Sir Eleanor! We are here for you!"

Their hearts leaped as the swords rocketed towards them.

Barely had the familiar pommels met their hands when their assailant gestured and tiny darts hissed out of the trees, striking them each in the throat. Odo felt a sting of pain, followed by a rushing, clouding sensation as darkness swept over him once more. The last thing he saw as he dropped to the ground was six more hooded figures stepping out of the trees, and Biter sweeping up to meet them.

Eleanor's second awakening in as many hours took much longer than the first, arriving in fits and starts like Pickles the cat approaching a stranger. She didn't even realize she was awake until she caught herself wondering if the smothering moths had just been a terrible dream . . . and

Egda's near-death experience . . . followed by the giant figure approaching them from the heart of the forest . . .

None of it had been a dream. It was all real.

Eleanor came to full wakefulness with a sudden jerk, sitting bolt upright and flinging what felt like a blanket from her legs. She was lying on a rush bed in a long, stone room lit only by a fire at one end. By that flickering light she made out a high, vaulted ceiling, tapestries of dragons in flight down the walls, and three sleeping figures lying on beds next to hers: Odo, Hundred, and Egda, all three snoring heavily.

She let out a sigh of partial relief. They were alive, somehow. But where were they? And what was going to happen to them next?

Her eyes adjusted further to the firelight and made out a sword stand in front of the fire. In it were two swords, conversing in low tones.

"Runnel!"

The topmost sword leaped from its rest on the stand and rushed to her. "Sir Eleanor! You have awoken at last."

"Yes, but I don't know . . . anything. What's going on? Where were you when we needed you?"

"That is either a very short or a very long story, depending on how you tell it." Runnel balanced on her tip and leaned close, so her ruby touched Eleanor on the arm. "My brother and I, we thought you were safe in the forest at the bottom of the Ghyll. We did not know about the moths, otherwise we would never have left you."

"But then that man in the woods . . ." Eleanor rubbed her neck, where a numb, upraised patch marked the spot the dart had struck her. "He attacked us."

"There is much we did not know."

A door opened and closed, and a hooded figure stepped into the room. Eleanor stood and raised Runnel before her.

"Stop there. Come not one step closer!"

The figure raised its hands straight up into the air. "I'm Adelind," it squeaked in the high-pitched voice of a startled girl around Eleanor's age, "third apprentice to Master Knucius. I mean you no harm."

Now that Eleanor studied the figure more closely, she could see that it was much shorter and more slender than the one she had seen in the woods. And when the girl called Adelind hesitantly tugged back her hood, revealing a thick mane of golden curls, messily tied back in a knot, she knew for certain that they were very different people. Adelind had a long, pointy nose and sprightly blue eyes, and though she had small spark scars on her face, there were far fewer than on the huge fellow in the forest.

"Where are we?" Eleanor asked her.

"C-Clynan Smithy. Your swords came to us for aid."

"And so you attacked us?"

"We only did as our charter demands. None but those who serve the forge — the true smith and apprentices — may know its location. Not even knights. We are honestly and terribly sorry to have frightened you."

"I . . . I wasn't frightened," said Eleanor. "I was just confused."

"Understandably so. All will be explained, I promise. Can I put my hands down now?"

"Yes, of course. Sorry."

"Are you feeling well? Your sleep was long and very deep. Can you stand?"

Eleanor tested her legs, as yet unwilling to let go of Runnel. Her knees held.

"Good," Adelind said. "Would you care to eat with us? We are about to have our evening meal."

"I'll wait for the others, if it's all the same to you." She still didn't entirely trust the situation and wasn't about to leave her friends alone for a second.

"They will wake soon. The fire in your veins roused you first, as Master Knucius predicted."

Eleanor checked on Odo, then Egda, then Hundred. They all seemed to be sleeping soundly. On the floor next to Egda's bed lay his staff and the small blade he used to cut up his meals, the only weapons he carried. Surrounding Hundred's bed . . .

Eleanor blinked, doubting her eyes.

All about Hundred's bed was a sea of silvery metal. Fixed blades, folding blades, blades that could be concealed in a collar, cuff, hem, or epaulette, or in the heels and toes and sides of boots. Knives for stabbing, sawing, slashing, and throwing. Needles, spikes, barbs, prickets — every deadly shape imaginable was present in unimaginable number.

"Ninety-nine," said Adelind, catching the direction of Eleanor's gaze.

"What?"

"That's how many weapons your friend was carrying. We have never seen such armament on a single person — all fashioned from the finest steel too. She is truly a bodyguard fit for a king."

Eleanor studied Adelind closely and was relieved to find nervousness and restless excitement, but no sign of ill intent. Still, it unnerved her to understand how exposed they were.

"You know who we are?"

"We told them," said Runnel. "We had to, in order to obtain their help."

"You mean they wouldn't have helped us anyway?" asked Odo from behind them. "They would have just left us there, maybe dying, because we weren't important enough?"

Odo rose to his feet and Biter swept into his waiting hand. He had woken a moment ago, and pretended to snore while taking stock of his surroundings. It didn't sound like Eleanor was in any danger, but it paid to be cautious. Who knew what sort of callous band they had fallen in with?

Literally *fallen*, he thought, remembering all too clearly the headlong plunge down the Ghyll. They had been lucky to survive twice that day already. He wasn't going to risk their fortune turning now.

"Oh dear," said Adelind, putting her hands up again. "You do not understand."

"So explain," said Hundred, also rising to her feet. She held her sword in one hand. "We are listening."

Adelind took a step back with another squeak.

"We mean only good, not harm!" she said.

"If that is so," said Egda with quiet authority, "then you have nothing to fear from us."

Adelind took in the four companions and their weapons with one nervously assessing glance, then lowered her hands.

"Perhaps . . . yes, it's almost certainly best that Master Knucius talk to you now. This way."

Turning quickly, she led them toward the door, which opened before her and guided them deeper into the smithy.

Master Knucius was the giant they had seen in the forest. He was no less impressive sitting at the end of a broad wooden table lined with steaming dishes. When Adelind brought the smithy's guests to him, he stood and indicated that they should sit in the empty positions around the table. There were five out of eleven. The rest were filled with men and women ranging from Adelind's age to around forty winters.

"These are my apprentices," said Master Knucius in a voice like ancient trees falling. "Snorri, Theudhar, Vragi, Childa, and Jorunn. Adelind you have already met. Welcome to Clynan Smithy, the last remaining true smithy in the Groanwood."

He bowed, and both Odo and Eleanor felt compelled to bow in return. Though these were the people who had shot them with darts and carried them to places unknown, there was something about the giant man that demanded deference. Hundred bowed too, although not so deeply. Only Egda remained upright, though he did bend his head.

"Please, sit," Knucius implored them. "Eat. You must be very hungry after your ordeal."

That was true. Odo's stomach rumbled at the scent of fresh bread, roasted meat, and numerous fragrant herbs. He glanced at Eleanor, who nodded tightly. Unless Hundred or Egda said otherwise, there was no obvious reason to be skeptical — of the food, at least. They would all be eating it.

Adelind poured ale. Knucius returned to his seat when Egda was in his. Odo felt the bright eyes of the apprentices watching him closely, and sensed a thousand questions waiting to be put to them.

"Why are you being so nice to us now?" he asked, getting in first. "After putting us to sleep with poison darts?"

"The smithy is secret," said the oldest apprentice, the man named Vragi. "No one can know where it is."

That accorded with what Adelind had said, but it wasn't the end of the issue. "Couldn't you have told us about it? Maybe you could have just blindfolded those of us who can see."

"There wasn't time," said the apprentice called Childa. "Guards were descending along the road at an unprecedented pace. Any hesitation would have been disastrous for all of us."

Hundred nodded as though she had expected this answer. "You covered your tracks well, I presume."

"Very well indeed," said Adelind with a grin.

"And how did you convince the guards that they found what they sought?"

"Four fresh pig carcasses," said Knucius in his bedrock-steady tones, "mangled beyond recognition. What the ruse did not require, we eat tonight."

He gestured at the bowls of meat. Odo identified trotters, ears, tails, and other parts of a pig that could not be mistaken for human no matter how "mangled" they were.

His stomach turned. Suddenly he wasn't hungry. The apprentices, however, seemed delighted by the unexpected feast.

"Are you really Egda the Old Dragon?" asked Snorri, the youngest male, as he scooped a couple of choice cuts onto his plate.

"I was." Egda sniffed. "Now I am just Egda."

"*Sir* Egda," Hundred firmly corrected him.

"And you're on your way to Winterset to thwart Regent Odelyn's plans to oust Prince Kendryk and finish getting rid of the knights and stewards?"

"You are well informed of the kingdom's affairs," Egda observed drily. "Would that I'd had your knowledge sooner."

"We send patrols all about us, to keep the smithy secret, and so learn the news from intercepted wanderers and the like," said Knucius. "Also, the farmsteads from whom we source provisions have all had Instruments imposed on them, with their greatly increased tithes, taxes, and tolls. They suffer, as all will suffer if Odelyn secures her grip upon the realm. Please, Jorunn, pass our guests the greens."

Eleanor took the bowl.

"What's a true smithy?" she asked. "And why is it so secret?"

The six apprentices went to answer at once and were silenced by a raised hand from their master.

"That is a harder question to answer than you realize," he said. "Much of the world's knowledge is dangerous and should not be shared widely. On the other hand, knowledge that is hidden is in constant danger of being lost. I am charged with preserving a pact that has existed for many centuries, ensuring that certain techniques do not fall into the wrong hands. One of my apprentices will carry on the tradition when I am gone. Thus Clynan Smithy has endured the ages, and will endure ages to come."

Odo glanced at Eleanor. She raised an eyebrow. The smith's reference to a pact had not gone unnoticed.

Knucius continued. "Suffice it to say that your faithful swords sensed the presence of Clynan Smithy in your time of need, and came immediately to us. They could have guided you here, through the Groanwood, but you were incapacitated. Once we learned who you were, we rushed to your aid."

That brought Odo back to his earlier concern. "And if we had not been knights and an Old Dragon and his bodyguard? Would you have left us there to die?"

"We would never have known you were there. Only your swords — magical swords that only knights can wield — could have found this place, and except in direst need we do not stray beyond our doorstep. This, in part, is how we have remained undiscovered for so long."

Eleanor supposed that made a kind of sense, although it troubled her if she pondered it too deeply. Had no one ever stumbled across the smithy by accident and told others of their discovery? How could something be so well hidden that it absolutely never could be found? Perhaps it was underground, or invisible . . .

"I think I met you once," Hundred told Knucius around a cheekful of gristle. "In Aern, after the great revolt. You were blacksmith to the king's guard."

"For a time, yes, I was. You have a good memory. That was many years ago." His deep-set eyes twinkled with fond recollections. "Your name was different then."

"I never put much store in names."

"No, I see that now."

Biter was buzzing at Odo's back, as though he wanted to ask something.

"Yes, Biter, go ahead."

"𝔈xcuse me, 𝔐aster 𝔖mith, but you have healed my knight and our siege. We will be forever grateful."

"I am honored to be of service." Knucius inclined his head. "Would that I could do more, but my duty lies here, not in the world beyond."

"𝔓erhaps there is something else you could do . . . for me . . . if it is not too much to ask."

"I know the boon you seek," said Knucius, and suddenly Odo did too.

Biter's nick, the sword's one tiny imperfection — no one knew what had caused it, and the smiths at Anfyltarn had been unable to repair it. Perhaps a *true* smith possessed the skill to make Biter whole.

"Only two things can harm an enchanted sword," Knucius said. "A dragon's tooth or another enchanted sword. Do you remember which caused your nick?"

"No," said Biter forlornly. "But I have long suspected that I was once a dragonslayer. If only I knew!"

"Does the nick itself plague you?" Knucius asked. "Or is it the mere thought of imperfection that causes you pain?"

It was a question that Biter did not immediately answer.

"Both, or so I believe," supplied Runnel. "My brother is undoubtedly vain, but he also suffers from ignorance. This might be connected to the nick, or to the centuries he spent at the bottom of a river —"

"Eels." Biter shuddered. "Would that I could forget them."

"I believe he would be a happier sword," Runnel concluded, "if he could remember."

"Would it please you for me to grant this boon?" Knucius asked Runnel. "Would it ease your burden?"

"I am no longer the Sorrowful Sword, Master Smith," she told him. "My curse is lifted. I serve Sir Eleanor, who I know will one day be a great knight, and my liege, but I do also care for my brother's well-being. We are siblings of the true smithy in Eathrylden. We are bound forever."

"Nobly said," the smith told her. "Very well. I will inspect the wound this evening, after our meal, and repair it if I can. This will bring me a rare opportunity to teach my apprentices more of the art of such blades." Heads bobbed eagerly around the table. "I would say one thing, however, in caution. Sometimes we forget things for a reason, humans and swords alike. Dragons too, although they would never admit it."

"The mighty Quenwulf charged us with learning more of our true natures," Biter said.

"Did she? Well, she has her reasons, I suppose."

He spoke with such familiarity that Eleanor asked, "Do you know her?"

"Distantly," he replied with a faint smile. "I owe my livelihood to a boon from her father."

On that subject, he would say no more. They passed the rest of the meal in conversation about smother-moths, barrow bats, gore yaks, bilewolves, and many other strange creatures awaiting the young knights in the wider world. If even half of the ones she hadn't met yet were real, Eleanor decided, the world was a very exciting — and dangerous — place indeed.

"Wait here until I come back," Adelind told them upon returning them to their room. "All except Biter. If you will come with me, good sword."

"Can't we watch?" asked Odo.

"No, the master said so," she said with calm finality. She seemed to have overcome her earlier nervousness. Odo wondered how often she saw strangers. Possibly rarely. "The secrets of the smithy can only be known to those sworn into its service."

That was a blow to Eleanor's curiosity, but not entirely unexpected. When Adelind and Biter were gone, she restlessly paced the room, tapping the four walls with the toes of her boots.

"What is it with this place?" she wondered for the hundredth time. "Have you noticed that there are no windows? Just lots of musty dragon tapestries."

Odo nodded. "I haven't seen any doors either. Not to the outside."

"Plenty of chimneys, though. I guess that's to let out any smoke from the forge."

"You guess correctly," said Egda. "I have been in one such smithy before. I was very young. My mother, the king, sent me to learn something of this secret tradition, just as I learned a little about many other secrets in the kingdom. That is one of the principal duties of a ruler: to know one's kingdom more thoroughly than anyone else."

"Which makes me wonder how young Kendryk has ended up where he has," Hundred said. "He was trained, wasn't he?"

"As well as any heir." Egda looked glum. "We either missed something, or the regent had her own secrets that she kept from us."

"My coin is on the latter."

Hundred began putting her many blades back into their pockets, while Eleanor watched in fascination.

Odo lay back on his bed, listening to the fire crackle. He wondered what was happening to Biter. Knucius would have to soften his steel in a furnace in order to repair the nick. He hoped they wouldn't have to melt him down completely and reforge him. Surely then he would be an entirely different sword, and it would take a long time.

"Do not be afraid for my brother," said Runnel, coming to hover next to him. "The smiths will do nothing to harm him."

"But what if he comes back . . . different?" asked Odo, voicing deeper fears. "What if he remembers something important from the past that he has left undone and doesn't want me to be his knight anymore?"

Eleanor crossed the room to punch his shoulder. "Don't be such a lubberwort. You're the one who woke him up, remember? He'd still be at the bottom of the Silverrun if it wasn't for you. He's not going to leave you behind just because he remembered a . . . I don't know, a girlfriend or boyfriend or something. Do swords have girlfriends or boyfriends, Runnel?"

"No," her sword said. "It is not in our natures to associate solely with our own kind."

"There you go, then. You're his knight, Sir Odo. He's not going to leave you for anyone."

"I hope not," he said, with a feeling of relief that surprised him. Although Odo hadn't wished to be a knight, he had learned to like the sense of accomplishment that came with it. He loved the satisfaction of doing a good day's work, as he had in the mill. Now he had new work, and he wanted to do it well.

"Hope for something more useful," Eleanor told him, "like a quick road to Winterset before the regent has her way."

Hundred started to say something, but was drowned out by a sudden roar. All eyes turned to face the door, half expecting a monster to burst in, but the door remained firmly shut. The roar persisted for several seconds, then subsided to a deep hiss through which loud pounding sounds could be heard. Hammers, Eleanor thought — but hammers unlike any she had ever known — followed by a screech of metal on metal that made her ears ring.

"It is the forge!" cried Egda over the terrible sound.

"What are they doing in there?" bellowed Odo.

"I do not know. Some things are secret even from kings!" There was no point talking any longer. They lay or paced or polished their weapons, as their individual temperaments dictated, and waited for the din to subside.

When, with one last earsplitting screech, the forge finally fell silent, Odo took the pillow off his head and sat up. The smithy seemed to shudder in the sudden absence of noise. He caught Eleanor's eye, hardly daring to breathe.

A thump at the door made them both jump. They were on their feet when it opened, eager for news of Biter's fate.

It was Adelind. "Come, Sir Odo," she said, gesturing for him to follow.

Her expression was unreadable, which only made the butterflies in his stomach worse.

"I want to come too," said Eleanor. "Odo's my friend. He might . . . need me."

"𝔄𝔫𝔡 𝔍," said Runnel. "𝔅𝔦𝔱𝔢𝔯 𝔪𝔞𝔶 𝔟𝔢 𝔰𝔬𝔪𝔢𝔱𝔥𝔦𝔫𝔤 𝔬𝔣 𝔞 𝔣𝔬𝔬𝔩, 𝔟𝔲𝔱 𝔥𝔢 𝔦𝔰 𝔪𝔶 𝔟𝔯𝔬𝔱𝔥𝔢𝔯."

"Very well," Adelind told them, "but no more. Swear that you will speak to no one of what you see."

"I swear," said Odo.

"And I," Eleanor said.

Adelind turned and led them out of the room, into a section of the smithy they hadn't visited before. Here too the ceilings were high and the spaces lit by blazing lamps or the occasional glowing stone, but the flagstone floor was appreciably older, with slabs bowed in the middle by the passage of many feet. The walls were stained black as though from blasts of fire and smoke. The only tapestries they saw were threadbare and partially burned. Apart from the roof high above, they saw no wood, and as elsewhere, no windows.

Adelind guided them to a workroom that was so hot Odo instantly broke into a heavy sweat. Benches lining the walls were stacked with what looked like large, dull gray trays in various semicircular shapes, many of them rather like kites, narrowing at one end to a near point. Bundles of long, curved sticks that might have been sled runners hung from the beams nearby. There was a powerful smell of charcoal and iron.

Biter lay on a broad stone table surrounded by Knucius and the apprentices. He wasn't moving.

"Is he . . . ?" Odo had to stop to swallow. "I mean, did you . . . ?"

"The nick is gone," said Knucius, and indeed there was no sign of it at all. The blade shone as though newly forged. Biter's emerald gleamed, and even the small dents in his golden hilt had been polished away.

"𝔥e looks . . . brand-new," said Runnel, with something approaching jealousy.

"In many ways, he is," said the smith. "He has been washed in sweet oils, bathed in three fires, hammered by a master smith. This will profoundly alter a sword. Is it any wonder he has not woken yet?"

"But he will, won't he?" asked Eleanor.

"I believe so." Knucius motioned them closer. "Calling to him may hasten his return. That is the reason I brought you here."

Eleanor could see the sense in that. It reminded her of the time Farmer Gladwine was kicked in the head by Pudding and, despite all her father's salves and balms, would only open his eyes when Mistress Nant offered him one of her legendary tarts.

Eleanor pressed through the apprentices and leaned over the sword. "Can you hear me, Biter? If you can, you'd better come back quickly. Sir Odo is forlorn without you. It's all I can do to get him to eat, and you don't want him to starve away to nothing, do you?"

Biter didn't stir.

Runnel tried next. Slipping out of her scabbard, she flew above the table, so her hilt pointed down towards Biter's.

"𝔏ittle 𝔟rother, awake. 𝔜ou have slept long enough. If you're not careful, the eels will get you again!"

Biter shivered minutely. The rattling sound of his blade on the stone gave them momentary hope, but he quickly fell still and did not move again.

Finally, Odo moved forward with a heavy heart, for what if Biter failed to wake no matter what he said? Sir Odo would be swordless in a world where knights were sorely needed.

"Biter, please wake up. The regent is taking over the kingdom and we must get Egda to Winterset so he can stop her. We can't do it without you. Everything started with you, remember? I wouldn't be here if we hadn't found you in the river. You can't leave us now."

"Not just when it's getting interesting," added Eleanor. "You'll miss out on all the fighting!"

Biter lay still and heavy on the stone slab, as though none of them had spoken.

"I am sorry," said Knucius. "I believe he will awake, but perhaps not in time. I can provide one of our ordinary swords for you, if that would serve your purpose. A pallask, perhaps, or a more elegant rapier?"

"Wait," Odo said, still thinking of Biter's long resting place at the bottom of Dragonfoot Hole. "There's one thing we haven't tried."

Reaching across the table, he ran the pad of his thumb down Biter's exceedingly sharp edge. Instantly, his skin parted and blood began to drip onto the stone.

Wincing, he raised the hand and squeezed his bleeding finger so crimson drops fell onto the repaired blade, running down the gutter just as they had when Odo had woken him the first time.

"𝔉lee, 𝔖ir 𝔑erian! 𝔉lee! 𝘐 𝘸𝘪𝘭𝘭 𝘴𝘢𝘷𝘦 𝘺𝘰𝘶!"

With that sudden cry, Biter swept up and off the slab. Smith, apprentices, Odo, and Eleanor dived for the floor as the sword slashed and stabbed empty air overhead as though fighting an invisible opponent. Biter recoiled from powerful blows in return. Sparks flew. He seemed to make ground, but then suddenly, propelled by nothing anyone could see, he flew across the room, ricocheted off the wall, and fell to the floor with a clatter and a ghastly cry.

"𝔑ooo-ooo!!"

Then all was still, and Odo, simultaneously hoping and fearing that the sword had lapsed back into sleep, crept closer to pat Biter's sharkskin grip.

"Don't be afraid, Biter," he said. "You're safe."

"Sir Odo?" said the sword, as though waking from a powerful dream. "For a moment, I thought you were my former knight . . . returned from the dead."

"Do you remember him now?" Eleanor asked. "Do you remember what happened to you?"

"I did . . . but it is fading quickly." Biter stirred in Odo's hand as though he might fly out again. "I see a terrible knight, clad entirely in black. She wields a terrible sword. We fight, Sir Nerian and I together. He is strong of heart, mighty of arm. I am fast. It seems that we might defeat our foe, until . . . behind the black knight I see an even darker shape . . . a shadow that grows taller . . . and wider . . . No!" cried the sword. "I can see no more. No more!"

"It's all right, Biter," Odo soothed. "You're fixed now. You don't have to remember any of this. It doesn't matter any longer. The only thing I care about is that you're back with us again."

"Your young knight speaks the truth," said Knucius. "Whatever you recall or don't recall, it is unlikely to have any bearing now."

"There is one thing," Biter told them in a steadier voice. "I remember the name of the sword I fought — the sword that killed Sir Nerian, I can only assume. That sword's name was Tredan Falconstone. Perhaps you know of him, Master Smith? If you can tell me that he has been lost or melted into slag, I will rest easier."

Knucius's ruddy face lost some of its color.

"I do know this sword," he said. "I know him very well. The smith who prenticed me was charged with erasing a similar injury to yours, a nick in the Falconstone's edge, but one that had grown worse with use over many years. My master knew the sword by reputation and attempted to melt him in the forge, but her ruse was discovered before she could complete the task. Still glowing orange with heat, Falconstone slew my master and escaped along with his knight — an equally damaged and dangerous individual. I have never seen either since, but I have heard of both, although they have changed their names. The sword is called the Butcher Blade of Winterset now, and his knight is Lord Deor, Chief Regulator of the realm, and the regent's right-hand man."

"𝕎𝕚𝕟𝕥𝕖𝕣𝕤𝕖𝕥, 𝕪𝕠𝕦 𝕤𝕒𝕪?" Biter's emerald gleamed brilliantly in the firelight.

"Yes, your destination." Knucius nodded. "But be wary, should you encounter the Falconstone. My master, before she died, was able to wrest free the black opal that adorned his hilt. I smashed that stone myself, hoping this might end the sword's grim intelligence, but all I achieved was to rob him of his voice — an act that appears to have driven him to even greater cruelty and malice. No sword that I know of, anywhere in the world, is more dangerous."

With that grim pronouncement, he crossed to one of the shelves lining the walls, took down four of the kite-shaped plates, and handed them to his guests. Odo and Eleanor realized that what they held were actually shields, shields that looked like leather but were metallic to the touch, and incredibly light. They were big enough to shield Eleanor from throat to knee, and Odo from throat to thigh.

"Take these," said Knucius. "You will need them if you encounter Falconstone. They were made from single dragon scales and will turn even the most deadly of blades."

Dragon scales? Eleanor examined her new shield in wonder. What were dragon scales doing in a smithy?

Odo was asking himself similar questions. Did that mean the tusklike shapes lining the walls were dragon claws, or even teeth?

"𝔗𝔥𝔞𝔫𝔨 𝔶𝔬𝔲, 𝔐𝔞𝔰𝔱𝔢𝔯 𝔖𝔪𝔦𝔱𝔥," said Biter on their behalf. "𝔚𝔢 𝔴𝔦𝔩𝔩 𝔣𝔦𝔫𝔡 𝔱𝔥𝔢 𝔉𝔞𝔩𝔠𝔬𝔫𝔰𝔱𝔬𝔫𝔢 𝔞𝔫𝔡 𝔢𝔫𝔡 𝔥𝔦𝔰 𝔟𝔲𝔱𝔠𝔥𝔢𝔯𝔶."

"Your true quest is to stop the regent," Knucius reminded the sword firmly.

"𝔒𝔫𝔢 𝔴𝔦𝔩𝔩 𝔩𝔦𝔨𝔢𝔩𝔶 𝔡𝔢𝔪𝔞𝔫𝔡 𝔱𝔥𝔢 𝔬𝔱𝔥𝔢𝔯," said Runnel.

"Indeed." The smith wiped his hands on his apron. "Return to your liege now and rest. You leave in the morning. I have arranged a sailing barge to take you to Winterset, ultimately along the Hyrst. You will arrive before nightfall."

He clapped his hands and the apprentices filed from the room. Eleanor and Odo followed Adelind back to their quarters, where they put a light bandage on Odo's thumb and relayed the events that had occurred.

"I remember Lord Deor," Egda said. "But the one I knew must be dead by now, and the title inherited by a cousin or some other relative, since he had no children. Or perhaps the regent simply chose to grant a stranger the title, rewarding them for their services. Or to secure those services."

"And those of the Falconstone," said Hundred.

"Yes, it would not be the first time a sword ruled its knight, rather than the other way around."

"Impossible!" said Eleanor, nudging Odo. "I can't imagine it."

Odo wasn't in the mood for jokes. The following night they might be in Winterset, and Biter was bent on a rematch with the sword that had notched him. Odo could tell from Biter's brooding silence that it was all he thought about. And if they survived that encounter, they would still have the regent to deal with. She sounded dangerous enough without a sword.

"Don't worry, Biter," he said. "We'll do everything we can to set things right for you. And if you remember anything else, you'll let us know?"

"Thank you, Sir Odo. Yes, I will. I still do not know how I ended up in the river for so long."

"At least you know now that Sir Merian didn't cast you aside," said Runnel. "That is one fear you can put to rest."

"But I could not save him," Biter said with some bitterness. "Surely he would have prevailed against any ordinary knight!"

There was no reassurance to be had on that part. Sometimes knights died, as Runnel knew well. She had lost three in a row. Eleanor could only hope that the runs of bad luck for both swords would end now.

After breaking their fast the next morning, Knucius and the apprentices took their visitors down a series of winding ramps deep into the earth. At the bottom, Eleanor and Odo were amazed to find a wharf carved from the stone, alongside which rushed an underground river, moving so quickly it was flecked with foam. Moored at the wharf was a barge with elegant orange sails, furled, onto which they loaded their armor and a small amount of supplies donated by the smithy. Its sole crew member, introduced as Captain Gnasset, welcomed them aboard with a grunt and gestured for them to stay out of the way. Vragi untied the mooring ropes and the other apprentices pushed the barge away from the dock while they said farewells over the echoing roar of the river and gave their thanks. But for the help of Knucius and his apprentices, they might have fallen into the hands of the regent, or much worse.

"Come back and visit one day!" Adelind called to Eleanor as the barge wallowed away. "It gets lonely here."

"I don't even know where 'here' is," said Eleanor. They hadn't once seen the outside of the smithy.

"Just send Runnel into the Groanwood to find us. She'll show you the way."

"Will you shoot me with a dart again if I do?" asked Odo, still grumpy about that.

"Only for fun." Adelind grinned and waved, then followed Knucius and the rest of the apprentices back up the ramp.

Eleanor waved back, then turned to look over the barge, staying well clear of Captain Gnasset, who stood at the stern, tiller in one hand. The long, flat-bottomed boat was called *Photine* and there was a cabin towards the stern for passengers, the deck at the front dedicated to cargo. It was stacked with boxes and barrels and sacks, covered with tarpaulins and roped down. No one would think it anything but a trader on a regular voyage down the river.

Photine was slow to get going, but once the current had her in its grip, she soon got up to a speed something akin to a slow walk. Gnasset rarely broke what appeared to be a vow of silence, at one point directing them gruffly to use poles to fend the barge off. The underground river ran through an artificial passage that had suffered several rockslides, and the way ahead was lit only by a lantern hanging from *Photine*'s snub-nosed prow. After several close calls, Odo was glad to see daylight ahead, then a diamond-shaped exit from the tunnel.

They rushed out of a mountainside on a raging swell of water that carried them rapidly under a thick canopy of trees. Branches met and tangled overhead like grasping fingers, hiding the sky above from view — along with any chance of seeing the secret underground river to the smithy.

With a rattle and snap, the mainsail rose and filled, Gnasset hauling on the halyard from her steering post at the stern. The barge was rigged to be sailed alone, and judging from her rare speech and general lack of interest in the others, Gnasset liked it that way. Probably the smiths had chosen the most reticent bargee they could find, one who would have no trouble keeping their secrets.

"This river is the Hyrst," said Egda, filling his lungs. "I have not smelled its fresh, cool scent for too long. My friends, now at last I truly feel as though we are coming home!"

Eleanor resisted the impulse to tell him that Winterset wasn't home for them, but a far-off place they had only heard about in stories. Still, she too felt excitement rising at the thought that they would soon stand where knights of old had been dubbed and had dueled each other, where heroes had lived and died, where wars had begun and ended. Her mother had passed through here, on the way to the battle that had earned her both honor and an honorable ending. Time would tell what fate had in store for Eleanor and Odo, but at least they were going somewhere *important*.

Odo measured the space between the cargo on the forward deck. There was a narrow lane between boxes, perfect for more knife practice, where they could stay hidden as well.

"Bored already, Sir Odo?" Hundred grinned as she tossed them each a blade.

Eleanor remembered all of Hundred's weapons laid out in the smithy. "Why ninety-nine weapons," she asked, "not a round hundred, since that's what you're called? Have you lost one?"

"Never. They only counted ninety-nine."

"You mean there's one they didn't find?"

"In a sense. There is one nobody can ever take from me."

"Short of killing you," said Egda.

"No one's managed that yet, my liege."

"The day is young." Egda smiled to himself as he turned into the cabin, leaving the hatch open so he could hear the knifeplay of the young knights and the rush of river water from *Photine*'s passage with equal clarity.

Eleanor worried at the mystery of Hundred's missing weapon while she and Odo reviewed the moves they had learned on the road to Kyles Frost. Did she have a spell she could call on in direst need? Or some kind of supernatural creature she was able to summon just once in her life? That would be a fine trick.

It was Odo who guessed the truth. He had been considering possibilities much nearer to his experience, such as Hundred's intelligence and knowledge of combat, her cunning, and her wit.

"It's you, isn't it?" he asked her while recovering his breath from a particularly close bout with Eleanor. "You're the hundredth weapon."

Hundred bowed. "At my lord's service."

"Who gave you that name?" Eleanor asked, kicking herself for not guessing before Odo.

"A master of fighting with only one's body. She trained me in the desert for three years, without weapons of any kind, except for the ones that I possess. She taught me that what makes the knight is not the sword . . . no offense," she added for Biter and Runnel's benefit. "But the spirit. If the spirit is strong, no enemy can defeat us."

"Even those armed with bows and arrows?" asked Egda, poking his head out to play the skeptic with wicked pleasure. "Or dragons?"

"My liege knows full well the difference between death and defeat," she said, unfazed. "That is why we are on this mission, is it not?"

Eleanor and Odo practiced all morning, getting used to their new dragon-scale shields as well as the knives. They broke off only when other vessels neared, or there were travelers on the riverbank who might catch a glimpse of them. Though Knucius had taken steps to make it look like they had died in the fall down the Ghyll, it wouldn't pay to advertise the presence of any knights sparring on their way to Winterset. So a family of traders they became again, eating lunch in the afternoon sun and taking turns watching from the bow of the barge for any debris or newly formed sandbanks. Save Egda, who stayed in the cabin, thinking deep thoughts.

The river became steadily wider as the day wore on, joining other tributaries rushing down from the mountains. Occasionally they saw huts or small boating communities and waved at the children who took delight in their passing. There was little traffic on or between either bank, and only one bridge, which required the mast to be unstepped and lowered, Gnasset dismissing the offer of help from Odo, skillfully using a mechanism of gears and pulleys to bring it down and raise it again.

Hundred remarked on the lack of traffic on both river

and riverbank, putting the blame on the regent, who had clamped down on the movement of Tofte's traders and raised tolls that made travel uneconomic. The state of the Hyrst River reflected the state of the kingdom as a whole, she feared, where short-term gain for the regent would be paid for by long-term disaster.

Once they spied a trio of disconsolate-looking knights hacking through an overgrown path on the eastern bank of the river. Their markings declared them to be from Nhaga, a prosperous province half to the east of Winterset as Lenburh was to the west. They looked tired and dusty.

"Nhagese knights," Hundred said to Egda. "They were ever among the most loyal, sire. Should we . . . ?"

"Do you recognize any?" asked Egda.

"One has the look and stature of Sir Haelf the Tall," replied Hundred. "A daughter . . . granddaughter, perhaps."

"Yes," said Egda, answering Hundred's unfinished question. "We may have need of them."

"Can you bring us closer to shore?" Hundred called to Gnasset, who shrugged but obeyed. "Within arrow range but outside the reach of a throwing knife. There."

Hundred stood up and waved her arms as the barge slowed, both wind and current weaker near the bank.

"Good knights!" she called. "Where head you?"

"Winterset!" called out a very tall woman with an accent that emphasized her *r*'s. "Spare us your offer of passage. We can't afford it."

"A knight short of coin? You must have fallen on hard times."

"Hard times indeed, for we have lost our lands and our livelihood. We go to petition the prince to reconsider his recent actions."

"Are you the rebels I've heard rumors of?"

"We are no rebels!" exclaimed one of the other knights, a man with a vivid scar under his chin, like a second mouth. "Our loyalty to the Crown is unquestioned!"

"Well then, penniless knights, would you consider a boon?" Hundred called back. "My father was a soldier. He had that same footsore look as you on returning from a campaign. Rest on a barge headed in the direction you're going will gain you much and cost me nothing."

The knights quickly conferred as the *Photine* grew nearer.

"Very well, we accept your offer with thanks," said the tall woman. "I can't deny it would be a blessing."

Gnasset brought the barge in to gently touch the shore. Odo helped the three knights aboard, and gave them their aliases: Hilda, Otto, and Ethel. The knights introduced themselves as Sir Uen (the scarred man), Sir Talorc, and Sir Brude (the tall woman). Sir Talorc had the breadth of a man but the voice of a woman, so Eleanor decided to think of her that way. They were road-worn, shedding dirt where they sat. When Uen removed his helmet and mail coif, a shower of pebbles rained to the deck.

"Sorry," he said. "We had to sell our horses and our march has been long, without a doubt. Your hailing us is the first bit of luck we've had for a week."

"Charity does not sit well with us, however," said Sir Talorc. "We would earn our way to Winterset, if you'd allow it. Find us a chore, or allow us to defend you if the pirates that have been known to ply the Hyrst River put in an appearance —"

"Rest assured," said Hundred, raising one hand for silence, "if the need arises, we will ask. Tell us what has befallen you. We are eager for news from the east."

The three knights spun a familiar tale: the arrival of Instruments from Winterset bringing new rules and demands for increased tithing, backed up by official documents and force. Unable to break her oath to the Crown, Sir Brude had capitulated first, then joined forces with Sir Uen and Sir Talorc from neighboring estates as word spread of similar misfortune. They had accordingly set forth to put their plight to Prince Kendryk himself, though they had also heard the rumors that he had been supplanted by his grandmother.

"Knights have been stewards of the land and its people for generations," said Sir Talorc. "We have served in peacetimes and war. We have given our lives countless times! Who are these Instruments to tell us we're no longer needed? On what grounds do these Regulators overturn centuries of tradition? By what right do the Adjustors plan to rule?"

"Some might say," said Hundred in a tone that made it clear she was playing devil's advocate, not espousing a true position, "that this system will be fairer than the old. It sweeps away the privileges of knighthood and replaces it with a hierarchy that is more accessible to all."

"Whoever said that would be spouting nonsense!" exclaimed Sir Uen. "I was born of peasant farmers, and gained my knighthood on the field of battle, as so many have done, or by adoption. Knights are present for all in need, and obey the ancient laws and customs. These Instruments follow no laws but new ones they make to their sole advantage, and they have the backing of either the prince or the regent to do it. If it is the regent, then she shall pay for . . . that is . . ."

He stopped talking as he realized he might have gone too far.

"There might be many other knights like you," said Odo. "If you all gathered together, you could form an army."

"A dangerous strategy," said Sir Brude. "One that would plunge the kingdom into civil war."

"Sometimes even a civil war is merited," said Sir Talorc glumly. "We hope it is the regent behind all this. If it is Prince Kendryk himself — the rightful king — I do not know what we can do. Leave the kingdom and become mercenaries, to die in the far west, I suppose."

"Your loyalty to the king is commendable," said Hundred. "What if we could prove to you that he is innocent, and it is indeed the regent who plagues the kingdom with these Instruments, Regulators, new taxes, and tolls?"

"I wish you could," said Sir Brude warily. "But where would you find such proof? What do river-plying merchants know of affairs of state?"

Hundred reached into a pocket and tossed her a silver penny. Sir Brude caught it and turned it over in her hand.

"What is this?" she asked.

"The proof you require," said Egda, emerging from the cabin.

He looked as regal as anyone could after a long trip through mountains and forests, battling beasts and enemies as he went. His gold blindfold, now facing outward again, was as straight as his back. His expression was as proud as his nose. Beside him, jewels gleaming, hung Biter and Runnel, floating points-up like a supernatural honor guard.

Sir Talorc gasped and lunged forward onto one knee. "Highness!"

The other two knights were quick to follow.

Egda waved them onto their feet. "A king no longer," he said. "I abdicated the throne, and I have sworn the same oath to the Crown as you, as a simple knight. My abdication was foolish, born of an excess of pride, as might also be said of my self-exile to the Temple of Midnight. But though I have been slow to return, I now go to mend matters and ensure my great-nephew sits upon the throne, not my treacherous sister. Are you with me?"

The three knights drew their swords and cried, "Yes!"

"Need I remind you, my liege, that we are being hunted?" Hundred said, but with a smile. "Pray resume your seats, friends, and let us make proper introductions."

EIGHTEEN

Biter's plan, of course, was to storm the palace as soon as they arrived. But only he believed that deposing the regent would be so simple. There was Lord Deor and his evil sword to consider, and the lighter of the craft-fires, not to mention a kingdom full of the regent's underlings.

Matters only became more complicated when, with a flutter of wings, Tip dropped out of the sky above, sensitive eyes blinking in the daylight.

"d! a! n! g! e! r! d! a! n! g! e! r!"

The three knights, seasoned by the return of the former king with two young knights and their magical swords, took a talking bat in their stride. The news Tip brought, however, made all give pause.

The coronation of the regent was scheduled for dawn the next morning. In the name of security, Lord Deor had ordered the Hyrst River gate closed and all visitors searched. There would be no entrance to the city by barge, not for Egda and his three friends.

"Roads too will be watched," said Hundred. "We won't get in that way either."

"Overland, perhaps?" suggested Sir Brude.

"That would take too long," said Egda. He pressed

his hands together and tapped the tips of his index fingers to his chin. "There must be another route . . ."

An idea occurred to Eleanor that she almost immediately dismissed.

"What about . . . no, that would be too dangerous."

"Tell us anyway," said Hundred.

"She eats danger for dinner, remember?" said Odo.

"Well, I was thinking of how we got out of Ablerhyll," Eleanor continued. "Through the urthkin tunnels. Shache said there were tunnels under every city, but then I remembered her telling us that humans aren't allowed in the undercities without permission, so unless we're going to fight the urthkin as well . . ."

She shrugged. It had seemed a good plan for an instant, but now everyone was staring at her with wide eyes, like she had gone mad.

"The pact does indeed forbid humans from entering urthkin territory uninvited," said Egda. "But the pact is broken. The normal rules do not apply."

"We can enter through the Shadow Way," said Hundred, "and petition the Monarch Below herself. If she grants us passage, we will avoid Lord Deor's precautions entirely."

"And come up on the regent from underneath," said Odo, clapping Eleanor on the back. "That's brilliant! Oh, except for the going underground part," he added, remembering how awful it had been the last time. "But apart from that, good thinking!"

Eleanor beamed at the praise.

"We would gladly accompany you into the undercity," said Sir Brude, speaking for her companions as well. "Might

I suggest, however, that instead we provide a diversion at the river gate, to ensure your safe passage through the Shadow Way? Both will certainly be watched."

Egda nodded. "That is a wise plan."

"The barge will reach the Hyrst River gate in an hour." Hundred looked up, taking in the darkening sky to the east. "Night will fall at the same time. We have that long to prepare. Eleanor — next time you have a good idea, do not keep it to yourself."

"Yes, sir. I mean no, sir, I won't. I promise."

Sir Brude winked at her. "Remember this day, young knight. A superior may never ask you for advice again."

The hour passed quickly. Odo and Eleanor donned their armor for the first time in days, and darkened its sheen with mud drawn from the riverbank, as did the others. Tip, after a fond welcome from Odo, scouted the way ahead, returning frequently to assure them that there were no obvious observers on either side of the river. Ahead, they could see the lights of Winterset proper, twinkling in the dusk. Each slow twist of the water brought them nearer to the capital.

Homes began to crowd the water, and *Photine* was joined by many other boats, the likes of which Odo had never seen. People of all shapes and colors swarmed the decks, calling to each other in unfamiliar accents. The speech of some of them was impossible to decipher. They might as well have been talking a different language!

"There," said Hundred, pointing at the port shore.

Gnasset guided *Photine* toward the bank.

Dimly through the gathering gloom Eleanor made out upraised pillars and partial arches standing out above thick undergrowth: the ruins of an ancient stone building, long left to neglect.

Photine bumped ashore and the two parties bade a soft farewell. Sirs Brude, Talorc, and Uen would go with Gnasset to the river gate, to sneak in and distract the guards watching the area around the Shadow Way. Odo hoped they would get through safely, and Gnasset and *Photine* would safely reach her normal berth. He liked the silent captain, and the knights were good, brave people he hoped to see again soon.

Hundred led the way along a narrow path through the undergrowth as the barge pushed off, its sail catching the evening breeze with a snap. The way ahead was still and quiet. There was no sign of watchers of either species, human or urthkin, but Eleanor didn't doubt they were there. The Shadow Way was the entrance to the secret undercity; people weren't going to be allowed to just wander in.

At a dense stand of bushes, Hundred silently urged them to stop and wait. Tip joined them, finding a handy branch at eye level. He quietly chirped that he too had seen no one nearby.

They sat and waited, making as little noise as possible, for perhaps an hour.

Then, suddenly, from the south came the warning blast of a horn, three times. Eleanor and Odo turned to face the source of the sound, although of course they could see nothing. The Hyrst River was much too far away, and by now the night was as dark as a tomb. Faintly, though, they thought they could hear shouting.

Egda alone had cocked his head in the opposite direction. Moments later, they heard what he heard: a crunching of twigs and leaves as two people moved away through the undergrowth. Guards, drawn to the aid of the river gate by the blowing of the horn.

The four of them shrank back into deeper shadows as the guards went by. Once they were safely past and their footfalls could no longer be heard, Tip fluttered off to make sure there were no more. He returned a moment later with the all clear.

"Follow closely," Hundred whispered to Eleanor and Odo. "Keep your swords sheathed. We leave our enemies behind us."

The ruins rose up to enfold them, and slowly the vegetation fell away. Their boots crunched on pebbles and flakes of slate. Hundred surrendered guidance of the party to Egda, who needed no light to follow the path. Sometimes he stopped to feel his way forward with the tip of his staff, or perhaps employ other senses, such as sound or smell. Once, he dropped to one knee and tasted a pinch of the earth. Satisfied, he led them on, Tip flying silently above.

Out of the ruins, a gaping archway appeared, the only intact structure Eleanor had yet seen. It had to be the Shadow Way itself, for Egda led them unhesitatingly inside.

Darkness swallowed them. Even sound seemed to fade away into nothing. Odo held his breath, not knowing if the walls were yards or inches away. Either way, the air itself pressed close and still, as though just opening his mouth might put him at risk of drowning.

Egda led them ten paces, then stopped.

"Stone make you strong," he said, bowing low. "Darkness clear your sight."

Four silver-veined figures, glowing from the inside out, stepped from the impenetrable shadows.

"Wide be your halls," said one. "Tunnels guide you true."

Instead of Shache's pleased tones on hearing the traditional honorific, this urthkin's response was thin with suspicion.

"Turn back, human travelers. This is not your path."

"But it is," said Egda, still bowing low. "We humbly seek an audience with the Monarch Below."

The urthkin hissed. "The scortwisa supreme takes no visitors of your kind, not after the breaking of the pact."

"It is on this matter I wish to speak with her."

"Your wishes are not her wishes, sky-dweller."

"They were once," said Egda, bowing deeper still. This was the urthkin equivalent of standing taller. "I am Egdalhurd Begimund Coren Theothelm of House Chlodochar, once King Above of the Human Realm and keeper of the pact between my people and yours. I do not demand audience, but I hope and believe that my old friend Thrieff will see me when she knows I am here, if you would be so good as to let her know."

The urthkin shifted anxiously and whispered among themselves in their thin voices. Eleanor kept her hand on Runnel's hilt in case things went badly, but she told herself that she had no reason to feel anxious. The urthkin had always treated them honorably in the past.

Something moved behind her and she felt a tiny pin-prick at her neck.

"Move, tall one, and I will spill your lifeblood to the dirt," said the urthkin holding the curved knife to her throat.

Eleanor froze, and her gaze flicked to her friends. Odo and Hundred too were each standing with an urthkin blade at their throat, visible in the glow of the hands that held them.

"Biter, no!" cried Odo, struggling to keep his sword from bursting free. "We are the intruders here. We stay or leave at their — what's the word?"

"Behest, I think," said Eleanor.

"Mercy might be better," said Hundred through gritted teeth.

"𝔗𝔥𝔢𝔶 𝔡𝔦𝔰𝔥𝔬𝔫𝔬𝔯 𝔶𝔬𝔲," said Biter. "𝔜𝔬𝔲 𝔞𝔯𝔢 𝔨𝔫𝔦𝔤𝔥𝔱𝔰 𝔬𝔣 𝔱𝔥𝔢 𝔯𝔢𝔞𝔩𝔪!"

"𝔗𝔥𝔦𝔰 𝔦𝔰 𝔫𝔬𝔱 𝔬𝔲𝔯 𝔯𝔢𝔞𝔩𝔪," Runnel reminded him.

Egda stood straighter, but not so straight that his head was higher than any of the urthkin.

"We await the Monarch Below's pleasure," he told them calmly.

"You will come with us," said the leader of the urthkin guards. "Say nothing unless spoken to. Touch nothing."

"We understand," said Egda. "Lead on."

Odo let himself be shoved forward. The urthkin at his back was so small she practically had to stand on tiptoes to reach his throat, but that didn't lessen the danger. It would be all too easy to kill them and bury the bodies where they would never be found.

As they shuffled forward along the Shadow Way, he felt the walls close in around him . . .

"w! i! t! h! y! o! u!" chirped a familiar voice from above, and he felt the band about his chest loosen a little. Tip was watching, one of many bats flying back and forth, snapping up cave insects — probably his family, left behind to seek out the former king. He would know if something happened to them now. That was some comfort in the dark.

They walked for what felt like hours, always downward, but sometimes turning left and right. Glowing patches in the walls enabled Eleanor to make out the rough edges of things around them, such as buildings fashioned from hollow stalagmites, doorways, even windows. Breezes touched her face from odd directions, sometimes tickling with the scent of far-off spices, sometimes slapping her with smells more foul than fair. She saw urthkin coming and going, and heard their soft voices along with rhythmic cries and banging that might have been music. Whereas the tunnels they had seen beneath Ablerhyll had seemed cramped and empty, Winterset's undercity was a thriving subterranean metropolis.

They came at last to a vast space that could not be measured by the eye. When Eleanor strained to make out the walls, she sensed only that they curved to her left and right without end. The ceiling rose up in a dome that never seemed to come down. Soft, echoing sounds filled the air.

Pale light glimmered. Somewhere nearby were many, many urthkin.

"Approach," called a sharp-edge voice from somewhere in front of them.

Odo's urthkin guard nudged him forward. He supposed that they had reached their destination, perhaps a throne room of some kind, and therefore expected to head up a flight of steps or another ramp to where the Monarch Below might be sitting. Instead he stumbled as the way ahead sloped sharply down.

A faintly shimmering crowd of urthkin hissed as the humans passed among them. Eleanor stubbornly hung her head, determined not to stand straight.

"That is close enough," said their guide. "Wait here."

Their guards melted away into the crowd, and Odo felt a thousand eyes staring at him, waiting for him to make a mistake. Remembering the stern instructions they had been given, he kept his mouth tightly closed, and hoped Eleanor would find the patience to do the same.

A single flame flickered into life several yards below them. It was tiny, dancing atop a narrow, white candle, but it seemed so bright it made them all blink.

By its light, they saw that they were standing in a barred cage on the edge of a wide, circular space at the very bottom of which sat a tiny urthkin on a low stool, a long crystal shard held upright in one hand, like a spear. She wore no crown, but Eleanor knew instantly that she was the Monarch. She sat at the lowest point of the throne room, perhaps the lowest in the city.

"I offer you the gift of light, old friend."

The Monarch's voice was thin, but strong.

"Would that I could accept it," said Egda, bowing his blindfolded head. "But my friends will be grateful."

"Your words are as fine as ever. Long has it been since you graced our halls."

"The loss is mine. In darkness I sought wisdom, but some would say I found only further foolishness."

"That remains to be seen. What brings you here? The pact offers no protection anymore; you have placed yourself in grave danger."

"I seek only safe passage through your realm."

"To what end?"

"To halt the coronation of my sister, tomorrow morning."

"You believe you are up to the measure of this task? You and your three companions?"

"I believe so."

"Then you are indeed a fool. Prince Kendryk could not stop her, and he was wiser than you, if too tall for any urthkin's liking."

"He inherited his mother's height, along with her birthright," said Egda with a fond smile that faded as fast as it came. "While Kendryk lives, I will hold out hope."

"And if he doesn't? My spies report that he survives, but a sly hand with a knife could easily fix that overnight."

"Odelyn would never kill her grandson. The future of her line depends on him producing an heir that she can control."

"Lord Deor might not see things so reasonably, and orders can so easily and tragically be misunderstood."

"You comprehend my haste, then."

The Monarch pondered Egda's words with her chin on one wrinkled hand, examining each of her visitors in turn. Odo tried not to fidget when she looked at him. There was something incredibly penetrating about her dark eyes.

When she spoke again, it was clear that she had made a decision. Unfortunately, it appeared to be the wrong one.

"I cannot interfere in surface affairs. The pact forbids it."

"But the pact is broken!" Eleanor cried out.

"Silence!" One of the guards reached into their cage and gripped her wrist tightly, yanking her arm so her face was mashed against cold iron bars.

Runnel was instantly in her other hand, and Hundred and Odo were close behind her with weapons drawn. Tip swooped down and flapped at the guard's face, but was batted away with one sharp-nailed hand.

"Harm any of us, and you will pay dearly," Hundred hissed in a fair impersonation of an urthkin's chilly tones.

"Desist at once!" The Monarch's command rang out through the vast bowl, echoing off distant walls and seeming to come back at them from all sides. The order was not just directed to the humans in her presence. Eleanor's arm was instantly released, and she fell back into the cage as suddenly as the guard who had held her retreated. Tip walked on his feet and wingtips to the base of the cage and climbed up to the top, where he hung, glaring angrily at any urthkin who approached.

"We are urthkin," the Monarch Below rebuked her fellows. "We do not injure those who come to us in honest supplication. Even if they are disrespectful. Human girl, step forward."

Eleanor obeyed, blushing furiously.

"The pact is indeed broken," the Monarch Below said. "Humans no longer trade fairly with urthkin. They talk of flooding the undercities. They creep into our tunnels to steal treasure they think we hoard. What would you have me do?"

Eleanor glanced at Hundred, who gestured encouragingly.

"I would listen to Egda," she said, "and give Prince Kendryk another chance. I don't know him . . . but he can't be that bad, can he? From what we've heard, it is the regent who has done everything, even when it has been in his name. He has never done anything directly himself."

"His time runs short," said the Monarch. "And my spies tell me he spends all his time finger painting. How will that save his kingdom?"

Eleanor had no good answer to that. Finger painting didn't sound very promising.

"We destroyed the backward weather vane in Ablerhyll," Odo said, braving the wrath of the urthkin to add the weight of his opinion to Eleanor's. "You know we honor the pact. Let us through and we'll do everything we can to set things right."

"Harm above means harm below?" said the Monarch. "Isn't that what we used to say, old friend?"

Egda bowed. "It has ever been so. War between our peoples benefits no one — and there will be war if Odelyn becomes King Above. She cares only about herself."

"Then I am decided," she said. "Your kingdom is in danger, humans. We will come to your aid. Our tunnels lead all under the city. You have but to tell us where you wish to go, and you will be taken there."

"We must be atop Old Dragon Stone by dawn tomorrow," Egda told her.

"That stone, of all stones?" she said.

"It is where our coronations take place. He or she who is to be crowned takes the royal sword and, crying out the ritual words, plunges the blade into the Stone. There is a niche for that purpose, carved long ago, some say by a dragon's tooth."

The Monarch Below nodded. "Our hammers cannot penetrate this rock. We can, however, take you to the base of Old Dragon Stone before night's end. Will that suffice?"

"It will do us very well, Majesty. Thank you."

"Thank me by putting a proper ruler on the throne you relinquished. If the young finger painter is not up to the task, find another."

nineteen

The Monarch Below gestured, and her guards opened the cage. Darkness descended once more with the snuffing of the candle. Odo felt strong hands urging him along, more respectfully than before, and he let himself be led, hoping that sooner rather than later he would be in the open air again.

They left the throne room and followed another complicated series of tunnels through the underground city, Tip flying patiently along with them. Occasionally, they stopped to rest, eating what little remained of the fruit, nuts, and bread the smiths had given them. On the second rest stop, Tip flapped around Odo's head, hinting that he was hungry. Odo put some pieces of fruit in one palm and held them out so the little bat could snatch them carefully with his claws.

There wasn't enough light to be sure, but Odo sensed his urthkin guide watching him closely, and when she spoke, he was certain of it.

"The winged mouse . . . we call them Friends in the Dark . . . he is your pet?"

"Tip? Not really. I guess he belongs to Prince Kendryk, if he belongs to anyone. He's helped us a lot, though."

"His kind help us too. They eat the eight-legs that plague us, and we use their droppings to grow crops."

"You have plants down here?" Odo couldn't believe his ears. How could anything grow without light?

"Yes, we have many. You should see the forests of — I do not remember your word."

"Mushrooms," Egda supplied.

"Yes, mushrooms. Some of them grow thirty arm-lengths high!"

"That sounds amazing. I wish I could see them," Odo said, with some honesty. "But how could I? There's no light."

"Ah, that is a sadness. Perhaps one day our monarch could make an exception for you, as she has made an exception today. You should bring your dark friend with you."

Odo held out some more food for Tip, who pounced on it with gratitude.

They walked until they were footsore and weary, through caverns and halls immeasurable to the human eye. They had no way of telling the time, which only made the thought of what lay ahead more unsettling. Would they have time to rest before taking on the entirety of Tofte's army, if it came to that?

"I do not expect we will face anything more than several dozen or so, without bows," Hundred said. "Although this coronation is real, we saw no banners on our approach to the city and heard no call for the population to celebrate. The regent will risk no public fuss until Prince Kendryk is safely dealt with."

"That's sneaky," said Eleanor.

"Many monarchs have been," said Runnel. "Gisila the first crowned her son in secret the moment he was born because she knew her uncle was trying to depose her. By the time he succeeded, the boy was grown into a man who knew the secret, that he had been king all along, and ordered his uncle executed."

"King Addlebert was crowned seventeen times," said Biter, "in order to confuse his enemies."

"Some would say that he was more confused than they were," said Runnel. "Permanently."

"It is difficult to be wise," said Egda, "when the whole world is watching you."

Eleanor could appreciate that. She didn't like it when even her father verbally quizzed her on her schooling. Answers she knew perfectly if she was on her own fled her mind with the ease of eels the moment he demanded them. That was why she left the judgment part of being a knight to Odo, whenever she could. How could she possibly know on the spot what the right answer was?

He told her once that he didn't really know for sure, but he did know what felt right, and he trusted his instinct.

That was the kind of instinct a king needed, she supposed.

And a willingness to trust one's ally in the dark.

At last, they came to the end of their long, subsurface journey. The smell of fresh rain wafted from an opening up ahead, and their guides slowed to a halt, calling out in their strange voices to the guards there. The urthkin parted before them, bowing, and Odo and Eleanor and the others crawled cautiously out of a narrow split in the earth and found themselves once again on the surface world, where they belonged. Even by starlight, everything seemed brightly lit, making them blink.

Odo let out a huge sigh of relief, which startled a sleeping parrot in a palm tree nearby. It squawked and irritably raised its brightly covered crest. Odo shushed it with an upraised hand.

"Where's the palace?" whispered Eleanor, taking in the forest of bizarre plants surrounding them. This didn't look anything like the capital as she had imagined it. Some of the plants were long and skinny, with a tuft of radiating leaves at the top. Others were squat and many-trunked, like lots of trees merged into one. The air smelled of flowers, of which there were plenty, and damp, which the ground underfoot definitely was. Slippery mud squelched as they moved for denser cover.

"Look up there," said Hundred, pointing. "That shadow? It's Old Dragon Stone."

Odo and Eleanor peered through the foliage. "That shadow" seemed to take up half the sky, an imposing, angular shape with a flat top. It was much higher than they had pictured.

"The palace is behind us. This is the Royal Physic Garden," said Egda, holding a star-shaped blossom to his sensitive nose. "If my mother had known that it contained a door to the undercity, she would never have let me play here as a child!"

"Doors go both ways — and I imagine this one will be sealed ere long," said Hundred, cautiously guiding them from tree to tree, closer to the base of the Stone. Their progress was slow and stealthy; they froze at the merest sound that might herald a human guard coming near. They could not be caught now, not when they were so close.

Even as Eleanor followed Hundred's gestured instructions, treading as lightly as a leaf in the older woman's footsteps, she marveled at the fact that they had arrived. They were in Winterset at last!

She couldn't see anything, and was sure that not every new knight dreamed of overthrowing a plot to take over the kingdom on their first day in the capital, but few people were as fortunate as her. That was for certain.

When they were just a few paces from the base of the Stone, which now loomed like a wall of utter blackness blocking out nearly all the sky, they stopped for a council of war.

"Our objective is simple," said Egda. "To stop Odelyn from being crowned, we must reach the top of Old Dragon Stone by dawn. Unfortunately, there is only one way up to the summit, and that is via the Long Stair. Given that large swithorm tree we just passed, I believe we are on the opposite side of the Stone."

"That is so, my liege," said Hundred.

"The Stair will be heavily guarded, which works to our advantage. No one will think to watch this side."

"But how does that help us?" asked Eleanor. "If the Stair is on the other side, that's where we need to be."

"A tricky approach by stairs," mused Biter. "Uphill all the way, confined to a narrow space so only one can fight at a time —"

"With enemy reinforcements constantly coming from

above and below?" said Runnel. "I believe it would be nothing less than suicide."

"Perhaps we could stagger our assaults," Biter went on. "Our fiercest fighter first, the remaining three at the base of the stair to fend off reinforcements, retreating as needed."

"You are forgetting arrows, little brother."

"Then we remain in pairs, with the second knight on the stairs to deflect shafts fired at the first. Our knights' new dragon-scale shields should be equal to the task. Why do you only see problems, sister, when I see opportunities for valor?"

"There is no valor in dying needlessly," said Hundred. "I would rather we all survived *and* the right person was crowned. To that end, we need another plan."

"Tip can fly up to the top," said Eleanor. "Does that help?"

"Sir Drust, it is said, once used a trained pigeon to break a castle siege," replied Egda. "The bird carried a thread to the top of the wall, passed it over a crenellation, and then carried the end back down to Sir Drust. Attached to the other end of the thread was a rope. As he drew the thread to him, the rope ascended, then descended, and once affixed to a tree stump gave him access to the battlements."

"Tip could do that," said Eleanor. "Or one of our swords."

"I have rope in my pack," said Hundred. "It should be long enough. Thread we can pull from our cloaks."

"Is there something Tip or the swords can loop it around?" Odo asked.

That question drew nothing but silence from those people who'd been to the top of Old Dragon Stone. Neither Egda nor Hundred could recall any extrusion strong enough to take the weight of an ascending knight, not in the form that a being without hands could manage, anyway.

"I'll go up the Long Stair on my own," said Eleanor. "I'm small. People don't even see me half the time."

"I doubt that would be possible," said Hundred, but Odo could see her calculating the odds. Unless he came up with another plan, that might be the only choice available to them.

"What about climbing the Stone on this side?" he asked.

"Much too difficult," Egda said. "I tried to scale it once when I was a limber lad. The cliff is too sheer. A laden knight couldn't climb ten feet."

"But what if we cut steps, somehow?"

"The stone is too tough for hammers and chisel."

"I know. You said only a dragon's tooth could mark it. But what about our swords? They can only be chipped by a dragon's tooth. Doesn't that make them almost as tough?"

"It does." Hundred pondered this further. "So one person ascending via handholds carved by the swords carries the rope, or a thread tied to their belt. When they reach the top, they can find an anchor point, tie a knot, and the rest can follow. Is this your suggestion, Sir Odo?"

"Yes," he said. "And I should do it, since it's my idea."

"No, you are too heavy," Hundred countered. "It should be me."

"It can't be you," said Eleanor. "You need to stay here

with Egda in case something goes wrong." She took a deep breath, imagining the gulf of empty air below her at the top of the Stone. "It has to be me. I'm the smallest, and therefore the lightest. I'll drag the thread behind me. I'll leave most of my armor here, but wear the shield on my back in case anyone sees me and tries to shoot me down. It's the only way."

Odo was amazed that his friend's nervousness didn't show in her voice. He knew how wary she was of heights, but all he could hear was determination.

"I believe this plan is not only the best we can come up with," said Egda, gripping her by the shoulder. "I firmly believe you can do it."

"Well done, Sir Eleanor." Hundred grinned. "Now, let us make haste. If we are to win the day, we must arrive before Odelyn does. And we have no way of knowing where she is right now."

TWENTY

Prince Kendryk swayed on his feet, staring blankly up the Long Stair like a man in a dream. The way was lit by torches, flickering and yellow. What was he doing here? Something important, he was sure of it. It had, however, momentarily slipped his mind . . .

"Get him moving," snapped a sharp voice. "I don't care if you have to carry him, Lord Deor, but we can't have him holding us up every time his thoughts wander. If he didn't have to sign his abdication, I'd have left him in the palace with his doodles."

The jagged hilt of an old, gore-stained sword jabbed him hard in the spine.

"Start climbing," growled the Chief Regulator in his ear. "Or I swear I'll push you in the back on the way down."

Oh, yes. Kendryk remembered now. He was ascending Old Dragon Stone with his grandmother for her coronation ceremony. How could he have forgotten that?

As his legs began to move, resuming his climb one stair at a time, more memories stirred. He hadn't slept for three straight days. That was why he had forgotten. And why hadn't he slept? Because he had been painting, painting furiously in the desperate hope of finishing in time.

Had he?

Had he finished?

Doubt became hope, which turned into certainty when a vision of the completed mural flashed into his mind.

He *had* finished. The great work of his life so far was done.

It was almost over.

Up and down his knees went as he ascended step by step, following a man he didn't know, a hairy behemoth wearing a wolfskin cloak and carrying a brand whose flames were green-tinged. Ahead of *him* was the woman carrying the crown in its ceremonial sack. There were four hundred and fifty-seven steps in the Long Stairs, a number he remembered learning from his great-uncle, who had taught him everything he needed to know to be a good king, except how to contain his grandmother's ambition. Nothing would satisfy her once she'd set her heart on the throne.

Well, Kendryk had soon thought, let her try. She'd quickly realize what a mistake it was.

There was nothing glamorous about ruling Tofte, as her procession of humorless, gray-faced Instruments, Regulators, and Adjustors proved. They had no life to them, no heart or imagination. Not like the knights they sought to replace.

His first move, were he king, would be to recall all of those she had sent out into the kingdom. He would have to find other uses for them, of course; it wasn't their fault she had deluded them with false dreams. They could help run the palace accounts, perhaps, or assist the lawyers negotiating trade deals with neighboring countries, while the knights went back to the manors. Yes, that could work.

Prince Kendryk's weary head spun with plans that utterly contradicted the reality he was caught in. He knew very well that he would never be king.

Step. Step. Step.

His hands were tender where an apologetic attendant had scrubbed them with a wire brush while two others dressed him in attire fit for the ceremony. There was still paint under his fingernails, though. When he raised his hands to his nose, he could smell the orange, the red, the gold . . .

"Remind me of the words, Lord Deor," he said.

"Which words?" came the gruff reply.

"Of the ritual. The ones my aunt will utter when she pierces Old Dragon Stone with the Royal Sword."

"You don't need to know," spat Deor.

"No matter," replied Kendryk dreamily. "I learned them too. 'Let Aldewrath object.' The great Aldewrath, who crowned the First King. What do you think would happen if he were alive now?"

Deor laughed. "Aldewrath was never real. Just a story for children. Like your daubs."

"I wonder if a legendary dragon ate my great-uncle," muttered Kendryk. "One old dragon eating another. Any more true tales of his death come along?"

"I'll feed *you* to a dragon if you don't shut up," said Lord Deor. But Kendryk was no longer listening. He was going up, up, up in the wake of a man who smelled of moss and rabbit droppings, while thinking of Egda and hoping the old man had somehow survived his third reported death. There was a smithy near Kyles Frost, one of the old ones. They would have helped him if he lived, Kendryk was sure of it.

Perhaps he was nearby, awaiting his chance.

Kendryk hoped so. He knew his great-uncle would want to be there.

Dragon, dragon, heed our call.

Come to aid us, one and all.

His lips forming the words of the ancient song, Prince Kendryk climbed grimly and in silence to a fate he could not avoid.

TWENTY-ONE

Just keep climbing, Eleanor told herself. *Don't look down. Don't even look up. Just reach for the next hand-hold and . . . pull.*

Her shoulders hurt, and so did her calves. Even the light cord she was dragging up tied to her waist had become heavier than she expected. But that was nothing compared to how it would feel if she fell. Briefly.

Fortunately, or perhaps unfortunately, there wasn't much light to see by. The city provided barely a glimmer as she ascended Old Dragon Stone, so even if she had looked down, she couldn't have estimated her height. She couldn't see the top either. It blurred into the black sky and seemed an infinite distance away. All she could do was search with her fingertips, seeking the notch that Biter or Runnel had hacked into the stone for her.

"l! e! f! t!" chirped Tip, and she adjusted her hand accordingly, found the spot. The bat's guidance was essential in the night; it was all too easy for Eleanor to drift sideways instead of going straight up to the next handholds.

Pull.

Her feet followed suit below, occupying the notches that had held her fingers not long ago. Periodically, one of the swords descended to tell her that she was making excellent progress, but she tried not to think about that either. She felt as though she had been climbing forever. It was easier if she accepted it and just kept going.

"r! i! g! h! t!"

Something tickled her face. Instinctively she blinked and twisted, while at the same time clinging tightly, afraid for an instant that she might lose her balance. It felt like a bug, perhaps even a spider!

Pull.

"If we make it to the top in one piece, it'll all be worth it," Eleanor told herself.

"𝔅rave heart, 𝔖ir 𝔈leanor!" called down Runnel, followed a second later by a shower of rock dust. "𝔜ou're nearly there!"

"Don't tease me," she said. "You've told me that before."

"𝔜es, but this time it is true," Biter declared. "𝔒ur endeavor has proved highly successful."

"Well, don't talk too soon. I'm not there yet."

Reach. Pull.

Far below, Odo strained his eyes to keep his friend in sight. Eleanor had long ago vanished into the dark bulk of the Old Dragon Stone. He reminded himself that this was a *good* thing. If neither he nor Hundred could see her, then neither could anyone else.

Fortunately for them, the sun would rise on the far side of the Stone. They hoped to climb in the predawn shadow, if only Eleanor reached the top in time.

The cord danced loosely in his hands as Eleanor took another step up. Odo carefully spooled it out, making sure it didn't tangle. As long as it kept going, he knew Eleanor was climbing.

"She must be near the top," whispered Hundred. "How much cord is left, Sir Odo?"

"A few fathoms. But she's still climbing."

Even as Odo spoke, the cord jerked back and forth in his hands. His heart froze, thinking Eleanor was about to fall, but then the cord began moving upward at a much more rapid pace. The spool uncoiled and then the heavier rope it was tied to began to rise, the great coil near Odo steadily unraveling.

"It's her!" Odo cried. "She's pulling up the rope!"

"Very well done, Sir Eleanor," said Hundred, beaming. "The hard part for her is over. Soon it will be our turn."

"Yes, of course." Odo checked the rope to make sure it too would rise without hindrance. "I should go last, just in case I slip. Not that I will, but I would hate to drag you two down with me if something went wrong."

"Very well." Hundred accepted the sense of his suggestion. "I will go first, then my liege. Unless he would like to be lifted up in a sling? There will be enough rope to form a rudimentary basket."

Egda barked a laugh. "You are mistaking me for our old friend Beremus. He was the one who had to be carried with his eyes tightly shut across Cheerless Chasm! Compared to that worn-out old rope bridge, this will be simple."

Odo grinned with them. It was good to see Egda remembering his old friends with happiness, not grief.

The rope ascended rapidly at first, then slowed as the weight of it increased. Odo was glad they had tested Eleanor's strength before sending her on the mission, otherwise he would worry that it would be too heavy for her to haul. The rope, fortunately, was thin and light, while at the same time incredibly strong. Odo had tested that element too, tugging on a length with all his strength. The rope hadn't so much as twisted.

They watched the rope ascend steadily for some minutes until, at last, it stopped. Odo gave Eleanor a minute to tie the knot, then gave it a firm tug, twice.

Two tugs came back down to him: the signal to ascend.

Hundred dusted her hands, gripped the rope, and began to climb. Odo watched her as she went up the side of Old Dragon Stone much faster than Eleanor had. The rope below her twitched violently in his hands, and soon it was Egda's turn to follow. He too was much spryer than an old person had any right to be, but Odo wasn't surprised. He had seen the pair in action too many times to be fooled by their looks.

When Hundred vanished from sight, the rope twitched two more times — a message relayed by Egda. A second later, Tip was with Odo, flapping excitedly to signal that it was his turn to join the aerial humans.

Saying a brief farewell to the pleasant greenery of the Royal Physic Garden, and trying not to notice an ashen shade to the sky, as though the first hint of day was already appearing on the other side of the Stone, Odo took the rope in both hands, placed his booted feet against the rock, and began to climb.

Above, Eleanor watched anxiously as her friends inched towards her. She was glad she didn't need to pull them up. After firmly knotting the rope around a sturdy-looking nub of rock shaped roughly like a horse's head tucked incon-spicuously into a hollow in the stone, she had bound her hands up in cloth to spare her scraped skin any further abuse. Just holding Runnel made her palm and fingers feel like they were on fire, even though the sword promised to be gentle. Eleanor wished she had some of her father's healing salve, but that was in her pack, which Odo was carrying, along with her armor.

She had a fine view of the western wing of the palace, a tangle of pointed spires and buttresses that defied easy navigation, but her attention wasn't fixed on it. Instead, every minute or so she leaned out as far as she dared to see how Hundred was faring. When she arrived at the top of the rope, Eleanor lent her a hand to come up into the hollow, where she dusted herself down and took a drink of water.

"Excellent spot," Hundred declared, craning her neck to see out of the hollow at the rippling surface of the top of the Stone. It was ridged like a giant fingerprint, press-ing up at the sky. "No one will see us until we want to be seen. Wait here for the others and I will scout around. Biter, with me."

"*Yes, sir.*"

With that, she was gone, scampering like a four-legged creature up to the very top of the Stone as easily as if she hadn't just climbed anywhere at all. Odo's magical sword followed like an obedient pet.

Egda was next, his staff tied securely at his back next to his shield, and Eleanor called down to him to let him know he was almost there. The former king needed no assistance joining her, however. He found his own security by hand and under foot, and stood with only slightly less flexibility than Hundred had.

"Hundred is scouting, I presume?" he asked.

"Yes, she told me to wait here."

"I have no doubt she will be back soon." He looked to the east, as though momentarily forgetting that he was blind. "Where stands the day? Is dawn far off?"

The sky was turning straw yellow over the bulge of the Stone's uneven summit. "Not long now," Eleanor told him. "Odo better get a move on, the lumpish . . . uh, knight."

Egda laughed. "No need to watch your tongue around me, Sir Eleanor. I have heard far worse on the battlefield."

"𝔥𝔢 𝔰𝔭𝔢𝔞𝔨𝔰 𝔱𝔥𝔢 𝔱𝔯𝔲𝔱𝔥," said Runnel. "𝔌𝔣 𝔴𝔬𝔯𝔡𝔰 𝔠𝔬𝔲𝔩𝔡 𝔴𝔬𝔲𝔫𝔡, 𝔌'𝔳𝔢 𝔥𝔢𝔞𝔯𝔡 𝔰𝔬𝔪𝔢 𝔱𝔥𝔞𝔱 𝔴𝔬𝔲𝔩𝔡 𝔱𝔞𝔨𝔢 𝔞 𝔥𝔢𝔞𝔡 𝔠𝔩𝔢𝔞𝔫 𝔬𝔣𝔣."

Hundred and Biter returned at the same time Odo and Tip completed their ascent. Odo had barely a moment to catch his breath while Eleanor quickly put her armor back on, with Hundred's help, and salved her hands. They needed to hurry.

"The royal procession has reached the top of the Stone," Hundred explained. "I do not see Odelyn yet, but there are Instruments gathering at the summit of the Long Stair. I have no doubt that she will arrive shortly."

"And I did not see the Falconstone," said Biter, sounding faintly disappointed that his nemesis wasn't immediately available to fight.

"Patience, little brother," Runnel cautioned.

"The ceremony will begin when they reach the proper place," said Egda. "Who is closer, them or us?"

"We are, by a fraction."

"Then we can afford to be cautious. They will move slowly, as one; we will disperse and be stealthy. In pairs, we can get close before they see us, and attack from two sides."

"Odo and Eleanor, together," said Hundred. "I will stay with my liege."

They nodded, relieved to be fighting at each other's side.

"Will you give us a signal?" Odo asked.

"We will use Tip, if he can bear the sun when it rises," said Egda. Tip chirped his assent. "He will deliver word that our attack is about to begin. Otherwise, use your best judgment — and ignore what anyone says before or during the ceremony. The words are mere tradition and mean nothing. Your task is to keep the crown off the regent's head."

"Get it to Prince Kendryk if you can," Hundred added. "We might as well crown him while we're at it."

"You saw him?" asked Egda.

"No, but he will be here. She will need him to formally abdicate his claim in front of witnesses."

"Indeed." Egda sighed. "Also, Odelyn loves to gloat."

"So, then, you have your orders," said Hundred to Eleanor and Odo.

"Stop the ceremony," said Odo.

"Prevent the coronation of an impostor," Biter said.

"Get the crown," said Eleanor.

"And restore peace to the realm," said Runnel. "A fine day's work!"

They split into pairs and headed off in opposite directions, Eleanor and Odo to the right with their magic swords, Egda, Hundred, and Tip to the left, staying crouched to avoid being seen too soon.

None of them noticed the eagle hovering high above, watching the humans scurrying, its once sharp, golden eye now clouded with smoke.

TWENTY-TWO

Ｈow many do you think there'll be?" asked Eleanor as they scrambled across the top of Old Dragon Stone, sword in one hand, shield in the other. Her raw hands were no concern now. All she felt was anticipation for battle.

"In her honor guard? Your guess is as good as mine." Not too many, Odo hoped, but he wasn't going to be put off by whatever he saw when they came into view. He had a job to do, and he would do it, or try to.

"Hundred made it sound like a lot." Eleanor was thinking strategy. "If they're only Instruments, like she says, that's a good thing. They're not the old king's guard — which is who we wanted to be, remember? When we were waiting for Sir Halfdan to introduce us to the court? Imagine if we had to fight them."

Odo hadn't thought of that, and felt relief flowering through his battle-ready nerves. If these Instruments were as hapless as the ones they had already met, the fight would be quickly over, no matter how many they had to face.

"They are still fellow Tofteans, though," he said. "Just like the people we fought in Lenburh. It would be better not to hurt them too badly, if we can avoid it."

"Fortunately for that plan," said Runnel, "I lost much of my edge hacking at stone so Sir Eleanor could climb."

"I do not call being blunted an asset," grumbled Biter. "I eagerly anticipate a good sharpening afterwards."

"You'll get it," promised Odo. "But until then, please try just to knock people on the heads, if you can. And not *too* hard, even if they are the bad guy —"

"Wait," said Eleanor, holding up a hand. "I see someone."

She dropped to her belly on the stone, and Odo did the same. He inched up beside her, straining to see what had caught her eye.

It was a pair of Instruments in red and silver, each holding their wide-brimmed cloth hats tightly to their heads. A strong breeze was making them awkwardly flop around. Fortunately, their animated brims had prevented them from seeing either of the knights creeping up on them.

"Back up," Odo whispered. "We're too close to them to get a good view of the whole party. Until we know where the regent is, there's no point attacking anyone."

Eleanor nodded, and together they shuffled around until the two Instruments were safely out of sight. They moved as quietly as they could, given armor, swords, and shields. As they swung around, relative to the wind, they began to hear voices carried on the breeze.

"Hurry that fool up, will you, Lord Deor?" a woman's voice commanded, taut with impatience. Surely the regent, Eleanor thought, but she couldn't see her yet. The voice could have come from just over the next ridge or from a great distance away. Maybe Egda could pinpoint them better.

Thinking of the other two, she looked up to see if Tip was visible. That might give her an idea of what progress Hundred and Egda were making.

There was a black dot some distance away. It *looked* like a bat in the predawn light, but it was behaving oddly. Instead of flying toward them or following someone below, it was corkscrewing up and down in a series of spirals, like it was drunk.

"Look," she said, pointing. "Something's going on."

Odo squinted. The light was getting steadily brighter. Dawn couldn't be far off now.

"That *is* Tip," he said. "But what's he doing?"

"It could be a sign of some kind, something we're supposed to figure out."

"It isn't anything I recognize," said Runnel.

"Nor I," said Biter. "Although bat signals have never had a traditional place in warfare."

"Wouldn't it be easier just to fly over and tell us?" Odo asked.

They puzzled over the problem for a frustrated second or two, weighing the mystery of what might be happening with Egda and Hundred against the need to get to the regent before the sun rose.

"We could split up," said Eleanor.

"No, I think we have to keep moving together," Odo decided, coming up on his hands and knees to peer ahead. He could make out a gathering directly in front of them, just a short dash away. Among two dozen or so Instruments were a handful of people in brighter garb, including a woman wearing an ornate sword on her hip. She had Egda's nose, marking her as a relative, and her purple robe featured the royal seal, so she had to be Regent Odelyn. Next to her was a strange-looking bearded man holding up a burning brand. The fire was greenish around the edges and seemed to shed no smoke . . .

"Craft-fire!" Odo hissed. "That's what's interfering with Tip!"

"He *is* trying to signal us!" Eleanor's heart leaped into her throat. "They want us to attack!"

"At last!" Biter was ready in Odo's hand as he jumped to his feet, Eleanor and Runnel beside him.

"Shields forward," Eleanor said. "Charge!"

"For the prince!" Odo cried.

Eleanor grinned widely. "For the prince!"

Heads whipped around to gape, but they didn't run more than two paces. From above and below, a swarm of animals attacked the two attackers.

An eagle and dozens of sparrows and rooks and pigeons swarmed from the sky. Scorpions, spiders, and ants issued from cracks in the rocks, crawling and thronging. They snapped. They screeched. Wide, ensorcelled eyes saw only their enemy: the two children in their midst.

For a terrifying instant, Eleanor felt as though she had been plunged into a nightmare. She raised her hands, covering her face with her shield and leaving Runnel to guide her blows, scattering the birds in a shower of feathers. Feeling crawling legs and furred bodies massing up her legs, she danced frantically to shake them off.

Odo was doing the same, but he knew that it was a losing strategy.

"Run!" he gasped. "Leave the small ones behind!"

They plowed through the swarm, and indeed the slowest of the creatures couldn't keep up. That left only the birds to worry about — and the Instruments who were already closing in with swords drawn, taking advantage of the young knights' distraction.

"Charge!" cried Eleanor again, thinking to use the birds to her own advantage. They were a blunt weapon, surely, unable at close range to tell the difference between knights and the Instruments. "For the prince!"

"For the prince!" Odo cried again, although he was mainly thinking of the four people the bilewolves had killed — Sir Halfdan, Bordan, Alia, and Halthor.

Eleanor and Odo ran into battle side by side, aiming right for the center of the pack. The birds came with them, angrily flapping and calling. Half the Instruments immediately turned and ran away, throwing their weapons aside, leaving just six to fend off the attackers. They braced themselves.

"For the prince!" came an answering cry from the other side of the royal procession.

And then a second. "For the prince!"

Hundred and Egda burst out from cover and attacked the backs of the watching Instruments. Two fell with throwing knives buried deep in their shoulders. Another two dropped with tendons cut in their ankles. Egda's staff spun, knocking black-clad men and women down in all directions while Hundred's sword cut graceful arcs through the air.

"Hold them back! Call reinforcements!" cried the regent, standing tall in the middle of her honor guard, with Lord Deor and the beast-master on either side. A lank-haired young man in a red tunic nearby had to be the prince. He was looking around wildly, startled by this unexpected development.

"Yield now," cried Egda, "and your treachery will be forgiven!"

"You're supposed to be dead, you old fool!" Odelyn responded. "How many attempts does it take?"

Eleanor and Odo concentrated on their own battles. Odo lowered the shield from his face long enough to block a wicked slash to his ribs from a skinny woman with surprising strength in her arms. The blow jarred every joint in the left side of his body, but he was ready with an answering blow. An upward swing of the flat of Biter's blade broke three of the fingers on her sword hand, and she fell back with a cry.

Eleanor had two opponents, one of them seemingly more afraid of the birds than he was of her. She soon showed him the error of his ways. A quick stab to his knee sent him to the ground, and she still had time to dispatch the eagle pecking at her ears.

"Think you're so clever, eh?" her remaining opponent goaded. "Anyone with a sword can be a knight. I had to pass an *exam*."

"Yeah? Well, examine this." Thinking of all the things Hundred and Egda had taught her on the road to Winterset, Eleanor thrust Runnel at his face, and he fell back in surprise. She took advantage of his momentary distraction to disarm him and then knock him out cold.

Stepping over his supine form, she batted away the birds long enough to take the measure of the battlefield. Hundred and Egda were on the far side, and Instruments were dropping all around them, felled from knives Hundred threw by the handful. Egda was advancing steadily on the regent, who was herself still moving, drawing a long tail of her honor guard behind her. She remained intent on her mission.

"I see the falconstone," Biter said in a determined tone, tugging at Odo to go fight him.

"Wait," Odo said, pulling him back. "We have to stop the coronation first. I don't see the crown." Wings and claws flapped at his face. "Ugh, these wretched birds! If only we could do something about them!"

Even as he said it, one of Hundred's blades caught the craft-worker. The bearded man went down with a cry, and his green-flamed torch went out. The animals were instantly released, including the scorpion Eleanor hadn't noticed raising its pincer to strike her throat. It dropped to the ground, turned a circle in confusion, and scurried away.

Odo gave a cry of triumph and raised Biter high.

"For Lenburh!"

"What?" Eleanor looked around and realized that Tip and the other beasts were no longer slave to a supernatural will — a will that had been permanently ended. "Oh, yes! For Sir Halfdan and the others!"

"𝕿𝖍𝖊 𝖇𝖆𝖙𝖙𝖑𝖊 𝖎𝖘 𝖋𝖆𝖗 𝖋𝖗𝖔𝖒 𝖜𝖔𝖓," Runnel cautioned as a furious Lord Deor shouted at the Instruments to attack and called for reinforcements from below. Those reinforcements came running up the steps, roaring, and Odo found himself separated from Eleanor despite his best efforts to get back to her. Hundred and Egda had also been driven apart.

"𝕯𝖎𝖛𝖎𝖉𝖊 𝖆𝖓𝖉 𝖈𝖔𝖓𝖖𝖚𝖊𝖗 — 𝖆𝖓 𝖔𝖇𝖛𝖎𝖔𝖚𝖘 𝖙𝖆𝖈𝖙𝖎𝖈," Runnel observed as Eleanor leaped over the supine form of another challenger.

"That's a game two can play," growled Eleanor, driving hard through the throng to where the regent and her pet lord stood. She was so quick charging through the lines of Instruments that only two managed to interpose themselves, and they were so startled to see a young girl charging them, wielding a magic sword, that the best they could manage was a token defense. She knocked them both down, and suddenly Eleanor found herself facing a much deadlier foe.

"Foolish child," said Lord Deor, raising his heavy sword. The hiss of its steel was as deadly as his smile. "You will pay for your insolence."

She didn't waste breath on words. Adopting the Third Proper Stance, she used the matching Deadly Strike, Angry Fox, to thrust Runnel towards the gap between Lord Deor's pauldron and gorget. This was one life she would not spare, if she could avoid it. But the Falconstone was faster than it looked, and swept across the Chief Regulator's body in a blur to block the blow. The deflection was so keen and swift that she hardly felt it. All she knew was that her momentum shifted and suddenly she was exposed down her right side and fighting for her life.

One blow she narrowly blocked, then another. Thankfully her shield proved up to the task, taking the force of the Falconstone instead of shattering, although her arm felt badly bruised and it took all her effort to remain on her feet. Cold sweat dripped into her eyes. Perhaps, she thought, she and Runnel had taken on more than they could handle, although she would never admit it. Grinding her teeth, she turned aside Lord Deor's next thrust and came in low for one of her own. Again, the Falconstone deflected Runnel with almost sinister ease, like it was toying with her, and she fell back under a rain of blows.

Lord Deor's smile grew wider still.

Eleanor squared her feet, and in the process looked down. Seeing one of Hundred's knives between her feet, inspiration came to her.

"Be ready," she told Runnel in a whisper.

"Always, Sir Eleanor."

She lunged forward and at the same time let go of Runnel and dropped into a roll, scooping up the knife as she went. Runnel completed the strike, which was blocked by the Falconstone. That left Lord Deor open on his right flank.

Eleanor leaped up and stabbed, adapting the Sixth Deadly Strike to work with the knife, as Hundred had shown her. The tip of the blade slipped through a gap in Lord Deor's armor, but he twisted away quickly enough to avoid a lethal injury. *Worth a try,* she thought, even as he landed a blow on her shield that would have split her in two like firewood had she not successfully blocked it; as it was, it completely numbed her arm. She raised the knife, knowing it was little use to her now. The Falconstone knocked Runnel aside as Lord Deor wound himself up for a blow that surely not even a dragon-scale shield could resist.

Then Egda was between them, his staff spinning a protective whirlwind around Eleanor, enabling her to catch her breath and her sword. Grateful, she squared up once more, and together she and Egda drove Lord Deor back.

"Where is the regent?" Egda asked her.

Eleanor didn't dare take her eyes off Lord Deor to look. "She was here a moment ago . . ."

"We must find her! She must not complete the ritual!"

Eleanor dropped back a pace, letting Egda defend her, and glanced around. The regent was hurrying away from the battle, dragging the unresisting prince along behind her as a hostage.

"Behind, to the right!" she told Egda.

"Go!"

Eleanor broke off, and Egda drove Lord Deor back several paces. In response, Lord Deor roared in anger — he was used to enemies fleeing, or trying to, not being forced back. And then Egda added insult to injury by turning and following Eleanor!

But even as Lord Deor started to lumber in pursuit, he was distracted by Hundred, who threw a knife that glanced off his shoulder without doing any harm. Another narrowly missed his ear. The third bit into his neck, and he turned with a snarl to see the small, old woman running towards him, sword held high. Her battle cry was wordless, a pure shriek of rage and blood.

Meanwhile, another voice triumphantly proclaimed, "Let Aldewrath object!"

The shout drew Odo's attention. In shock and dismay he saw the regent standing astride the hilt of a ceremonial sword buried deep in the Stone, raising a golden crown high, ready to make herself king of Tofte.

TWENTY-THREE

It was all happening so quickly, Kendryk could hardly keep up, particularly in his exhausted state. First, a swarm of birds and other creatures had descended on Old Dragon Stone, summoned by the unnatural fire carried by the hairy man. Then the honor guard had come under attack by none other than Egda and his loyal retainer, the legendary woman with one hundred weapons. Kendryk could have cheered, but then his grandmother had grabbed the small bag made of woven gold from a nearby Instrument and dragged him away from the fight, still pursuing her quest to make herself ruler of all she could see.

She could see a long way from the top of Old Dragon Stone.

"It's here somewhere," she muttered, eyes searching the well-worn stone ahead. "Ah, at last!"

The notch could have been a perfectly innocent crack caused by years of weathering or a lightning strike but for the ring of symbols surrounding it. Kendryk couldn't read them — no one could, not even the scribes who had recorded their secrets in the royal library — but to his feverish eyes they had the look of a warning. Or a promise.

"Stand still," she said, releasing him. He didn't run. This was exactly where he needed to be.

She approached the hole in the stone, drawing the crown from the golden bag and the Royal Sword from its scabbard. They had once been plain but valuable things, the products of a simpler time. Both had since been decorated by less secure dynasties with jewels, filigree, and etchings proclaiming the worth of the bearer — all of it unnecessary for the purpose they served. *The righteous ruler makes the crown*, someone had written in a book only Kendryk had read for hundreds of years, *just as the true knight makes the sword.*

"This is wrong, Grandmother," Kendryk told her wearily.

"This is statecraft. Weaken your enemies and take what ought to be yours."

"You have only made your enemies stronger. Don't you see? Your Instruments are hated across the land."

"They do not need to be liked. They just need to be loyal."

"They are — as long as you can pay them. What happens when you run out of money, or their greed rises to match yours?"

"Pah! I don't have time for this. We can argue politics in your dungeon cell — if I can spare the time from being king."

She raised the sword and slid it one-handed into the stone, completing the first part of the coronation ritual.

"Let Aldewrath object!"

Kendryk's breath caught in his throat. So quickly. All it took now was for the crown to descend on Regent Odelyn's head. Then she would be king in all but right and the land would tremble under her.

Unless something stopped her, at the very last.

Closing his eyes, Kendryk opened his throat and began to sing.

"Dragon, dragon, heed our call . . ."

The prince's mellow, surprisingly deep voice cut through the moment of shock that spread across the battlefield. Eleanor was caught midstep as she realized that the regent was about to win. Odo had just felled his last opponent. Hundred would have thrown a knife to stop the regent, but the only blade she had left was her sword, and that did not throw well.

Egda cocked his head at the sound of his great-nephew's voice, and listened.

> *Come to aid us, one and all.*
> *From a cruel and dreadful fate,*
> *Save us now, ere it's too late.*

Old Dragon Stone raised no objection to the sword or to Regent Odelyn's words.

She raised the crown higher and cackled triumphantly.

The prince kept singing, louder.

DRAGON, DRAGON, HEED OUR CALL.
COME TO AID US, ONE AND ALL.

His voice rang out across the battlefield and across the city. Bakers stopped with their hands in their ovens at the sound of it. Children stirred in their sleep. As dawn touched the slender spires of the palace, Kendryk's voice followed.

FROM A CRUEL AND DREADFUL FATE,
SAVE US NOW —

Out of the palace came the sound of bells ringing, glass smashing, and stone blocks shifting in their ancient seats. Heads turned to look as a cloud of color burst from every window and crack, rising up into the sky. There it swirled and stirred, a mix of reds, oranges, and golds, painted gloriously in the light of the rising sun. For a moment it looked as though it might disperse, but then it steadied and took shape.

A dragon . . . in the exact shape of the prince's mural.

Kendryk smiled to see it. All these weeks of labor had not been for naught!

His creation's ethereal wings flapped once, twice, driving the magically animated paint towards the top of Old Dragon Stone. Everyone seeing it quailed, thinking the magical beast might open its giant jaws and eat them, or wrest them up into the sky in its claws.

Even Odo and Eleanor, who had just a month ago braved the stare of the mighty Quenwulf, felt their jaws open in amazement and fear.

Odelyn paused, staring herself, a look of horror on her face as it seemed she was to be thwarted at the last moment by the grandson she had considered a fool and a dragon she had believed to be mythical.

But this dragon was flying too low. The broad wings flapped almost carelessly a third and final time. Then, with a soundless crash that somehow made the stone quiver faintly underfoot, it struck the vertical cliff face and became a mural once more . . . a portrait of a dragon big enough for all the city to see.

All was silent again.

A moment later, Odelyn released a short, barking, sarcastic laugh.

"Thank you, Grandson. A . . . a noble display," said the regent. "Truly fit for a king."

Kendryk did not reply. He stood there calmly, as if he was still waiting for something else to happen.

Odelyn began to lower the crown onto her own head, beaming a triumphant smile.

A smile that suddenly faltered as the stone shook beneath them, far more powerfully than it had the first time.

The regent stumbled and missed her head. Quickly, she raised the crown to try again.

Old Dragon Stone rocked a third time, even more strongly, as though struck by an impossible blow.

The regent staggered. Everyone did. It was as though the world moved beneath their feet.

"What's happening?" Eleanor gasped.

Odo shook his head.

"I don't know. Maybe something to do with that . . . ghost dragon or whatever it was . . ."

"Look at the prince!" she pointed.

Kendryk had exploded out of his patient pose. He was turning circles in place, dancing a jig that took him nowhere. His robe flapped around him as he clapped his hands in delight.

"What have you done?" the regent shouted, crown momentarily forgotten. "What have you done!"

"Called for help," the prince replied. "And it worked!"

Odelyn roared with anger and lifted the crown again, but before she could settle it on her head, Old Dragon Stone kicked like an egg with an impatient chick. A crack opened up between the regent and her grandson, and both staggered back from a jet of potent heat that issued from it. Pale blue flames leaped high into the air. There came a roar like the Foss in full flow.

"Who summons me?" The voice was so deep and forceful just the sound of it opened more fiery cracks in Old Dragon Stone. "Who disturbs my slumber?"

"It is I, oh Aldewrath!" cried Kendryk delightedly, even though the hem of his robe was on fire. He stamped it out. "It takes a dragon to summon a dragon — and you are the *original* Old Dragon. Awaken and repel the usurper!"

The crack at Kendryk's feet broadened, gaping many yards wide. He fell back with one arm upraised to protect his eyes. The regent stood gaping as the snout and chin of a giant, red-scaled creature rose up out of the crack and sniffed the air.

"It *is* a dragon!" Eleanor cried.

"Not just any dragon," said Hundred with awe in her voice. "That's Aldewrath himself!"

"I thought . . . I thought he was a myth," whimpered a nearby Instrument, who had dropped her sword in shock.

"Apparently not," said Odo. "Your prince just summoned him."

The Instrument turned tail and fled, taking with her those few who remained standing.

Aldewrath's giant nostrils opened again, sucking in mighty lungfuls of air, staggering everyone but usefully starving several fires of oxygen, so they went out. The entire top of Old Dragon Stone was covered in cracks now, and all of them radiated heat in waves.

"None of you smell true," Aldewrath declared, his vast head rising on a long, sinuous neck so one golden eye could take in Kendryk and the other his grandmother. "What has become of the kingdom?"

"There's nothing wrong with the kingdom," objected Odelyn, drawing herself up and once again raising the crown. She did not lack courage. "The only thing it lacks is a king — me!"

Aldewrath narrowed his lips, and his sinuous, forked tongue whisked across and wrenched the crown from her hands and tumbled it across the top of the Stone. Egda's head turned to follow the metallic ringing sound it made. A quick thrust with his staff stopped it from rolling off the edge and falling to the earth far below.

"Only descendants of the First King may hold the throne," roared Aldewrath. "That is the pact I made with her, long ago. I can be roused to protect the kingdom, but only by one of the First King's descendants. I carefully check when they follow the ritual during their coronation. In return, I am allowed to sleep in peace, without fear of disturbance from wandering knights and the like. As I am being disturbed now. Who must I punish for breaking the pact?"

Kendryk went down on his knees before the great dragon, but quickly sprang up again, because the stone was too hot.

"To punish the person responsible, you would have to travel back in time," he said, "and I fear that might be beyond even you, great Aldewrath! King Brandar the Wise lived and died three hundred years ago. He lied about being an illegitimate son of the previous king, and won a war to prove it. When he came up here to be crowned, you, great Aldewrath, didn't object, because you were even more deeply asleep than usual. King Brandar was a powerful sorcerer who tricked his way onto the throne and made certain you never woke up to reject his claim — and then he convinced everyone you were just a myth!"

"A myth? For three hundred years? That is powerful sorcery indeed. And treachery. But it does explain your unexpected scent."

"What nonsense," the regent scoffed. "Don't listen to him, Aldewrath. He's a madman. He's concocted this story merely to put himself on the throne —"

"Don't you understand, Grandmother?" Kendryk said. "I'm no madman — but if you can't rule, neither can I. None of our line can. We're all pretenders — even Great-Uncle Egda!"

Eleanor glanced at the former king, who held the crown reverently in his left hand, perhaps remembering when he had once worn it. His face was ashen.

"Not . . . king?" he said.

"You were crowned," Hundred reminded him firmly. "You ruled. What does a bit of blood matter?"

"Ask the dragon!" he snapped. "Maybe the First King's courage would not have failed, as mine did."

"I have no opinion under the pact I made," said Aldewrath. "If I have slept three hundred years and missed the end of my old friend's line, I see no reason to stay awake now."

The giant head began to sink back into the rift.

"You can't go back to sleep," said Kendryk, aghast. "You have to put *someone* on the throne!"

"I *can't? I have to?*" the dragon roared, eyes widening in outrage. Thin lips pulled back from teeth like long knives, and Aldewrath opened his mighty jaws wider, as though considering snapping Kendryk up. "The pact has ended. I care not how you decide now. Let it be the person who first wears the crown, for all it matters to me!"

With that, Aldewrath retreated into Old Dragon Stone, which shook and complained in response. Flames and smoke spurted out of the cracks.

All eyes turned to the crown held limply in Egda's hand.

Give it to me, brother," said Odelyn, advancing with a murderous look.

Eleanor and Odo closed ranks in front of Egda. Hundred moved to intercept Odelyn, and was confronted by Lord Deor. For a moment, there was a stalemate, with Kendryk standing helplessly to one side.

"This isn't what I planned," he despaired. "Aldewrath was supposed to honor the pact and choose a new monarch. Surely there's someone left in Tofte with the royal blood!"

"What does it matter?" his grandmother snapped at him. "Blood is no substitute for ambition."

"And ambition is no substitute for ability," Hundred retorted. "You are sending your Instruments out into the kingdom knowing nothing about the people or the lands they are to be stewards of."

"What's there to know? My subjects are the ones who need to understand that things are different now. The old ways are gone. No one believes in them anyway."

"That's not true!" Eleanor declared. "I believe in them. I've spent my whole life dreaming of being a knight, and now that I am one, you're not taking that from me!"

"See?" said Odo. "You know nothing about Tofte. You've never visited the villages and smithies like Kendryk has, and Egda before him. You've lived *your* life in the palace, dreaming of sitting in a fancy chair and believing that made you king. It doesn't. You have to earn it."

"I *have* earned it." Odelyn lunged forward, pointing at Egda. Odo and Eleanor crossed swords to prevent her coming any closer. "I stood in *his* shadow and watched him grow weak and cowardly. What kind of king just gives up?"

"She's right," said Egda. "I was not a good king."

"My liege," said Hundred. "Don't listen to her —"

"But Odelyn would be a worse king still." Egda raised the crown over a seething crack next to him. "I should drop this right now and let it melt!"

"No!" cried Kendryk and Odelyn at the same time. Lord Deor lunged, knocking Hundred back into Egda — whose fingers snapped open accidentally, letting the crown go.

The impact knocked the crown away from the crack. With a penetrating chime, it struck the stone and bounced across the top of Old Dragon Stone, rolling at a rapid speed.

Everyone moved at once: Odelyn and Kendryk for the crown, Hundred to save Egda, who was teetering on the edge of the crack, Eleanor to protect Kendryk, and Odo to block Lord Deor. Only Odo wasn't the only one choosing his direction. Biter was pulling him too, hoping for a chance to even the score against Falconstone, the Butcher Blade of Winterset.

"Out of my way, boy," Lord Deor growled. He was bleeding from a wound in his side, but it didn't seem to slow him.

"𝕾𝔦𝔯 𝕺𝔡𝔬 𝔴𝔦𝔩𝔩 𝔫𝔬𝔱 𝔟𝔢 𝔰𝔭𝔬𝔨𝔢𝔫 𝔱𝔬 𝔱𝔥𝔞𝔱 𝔴𝔞𝔶," Biter responded, ready to fight.

But Odo reined him in, thinking fast. He didn't fancy his chances against an experienced knight and his equally vicious sword, although he would fight to protect Egda. He was about the same size as Lord Deor.

"It's in your best interest to stay back, good knight," Odo said, watching the Falconstone closely for any sudden lunges. "You and I, we're just following orders. In a moment this'll all be sorted out, without bloodshed, and we can go back to being on the same side, like we were before."

"I'm not a knight, and I'm not on your side," Lord Deor said, his brows darkening. "I'm the Chief Regulator!"

With that, he struck, the Falconstone's black tip slashing horizontally through the air. Biter and Odo moved as one to defend themselves with the Fourth Certain Block. Metal rang against metal, and then again as Odo struck in return. He was used to fighting Eleanor, who was faster than him. Lord Deor was faster still — and Odo was very conscious of the fact that the Regulator was only the second person he had ever fought armed with a magical sword. Ædroth, sword of the false knight Sir Saskia, had been perfectly ordinary, and still she had beaten him.

That, however, was a long time ago and far away. Then, he had fought for his honor. Now, he was fighting for the entire country — and for his life.

Ninth Deadly Strike, he told himself, drawing Biter back for another series of blows and adjusting the weight of his dragon-scale shield. Chief Regulator or not, Lord Deor was just another knight, and knights could be beaten.

Eleanor saw Odo fighting Lord Deor but had no time to feel more than a flash of concern. At least she had weakened him for Odo.

Her outstretched fingertips had just touched the rolling crown when a strong hand gripped her trailing leg, and she fell over, almost landing face-first. Eleanor cursed and lashed out as Odelyn ran by, but succeeded only in tearing off a handful of purple robe. Using a word that she'd never thought to utter in the presence of royalty, she looked around for Kendryk. He was too far away.

Odelyn had caught up with the crown. In a moment she would scoop it up and declare herself king. They had all heard the dragon's decree. Putting the crown on her head really *would* make her king.

A black shape descended from the sky. Tip caught the rolling crown with both feet and furiously flapped his webbed wings. Eleanor cheered, but her relief was short-lived. The crown was too heavy for the little bat, and Odelyn too speedy. The regent got one hand on the circlet, sending Tip tumbling away and ripping it free.

With a cry of triumph, she raised it high.

Scrambling to her feet, Eleanor drew back her sword-arm and launched Runnel in a wild, desperate throw.

The sword flew true, darting with a whistle between

Odelyn's upraised hands, and caught the crown against Runnel's cross-guard.

"Cursed thing!" Odelyn snatched at the sword and almost lost her fingers for the effort. Runnel swooped around her, intending to bring the crown to Eleanor.

"No, to Prince Kendryk!" she cried.

Runnel changed course, and Kendryk raised his hands and ran backward to catch the crown as it dropped down from on high. At the last moment, a fallen Instrument who had been feigning unconsciousness rose up onto hands and knees behind the prince and tripped him. The crown landed in front of her, and she snatched it up in both hands.

"To me!" cried Odelyn, opening her arms. "Throw truly and I'll reward you with a hundred gold nobles."

"Only a hundred gold nobles?" the Instrument said with a sneer. "I heard what that dragon said. Anyone who wears this thing can be king — so why not me?"

"Why not you? Because crown or not, I'll have you hung, drawn, and quartered, you treacherous cur, that's why!"

Odelyn bared her teeth and began to run.

Startled, the Instrument turned and fled, the crown dangling in her left hand.

Odo blocked another powerful blow from Lord Deor. The Falconstone's keen blade skidded down Biter's blunter edge, stopping at the cross-guard with the force of a punch. Gasping for air, Odo pushed with his shield and forced Lord Deor onto his back foot. That was the most ground he could gain, but surely the older man's strength would have to ebb soon. Blood still flowed freely down his side, and his smile was looking forced. What Odo couldn't win by skill alone, he might yet take with superior endurance.

Distraction came from an unexpected quarter. "Leave this one to me," cried Hundred, kicking Lord Deor in the knee and breaking the stalemate. "Go after the crown. You have longer legs!"

Odo shook sweat from his eyes and looked around. Egda stood alone but out of harm's way, for the moment. Eleanor, Kendryk, Odelyn, and Tip were chasing an Instrument who was running for the Long Stair, dodging and weaving around smoking cracks as she went. Her current path took her not far from him, and in her hand was the crown!

Lowering his head and roaring like a bull, he ran, wishing for Eleanor's speed. But intimidation might do, and the sight of him had the desired effect.

The Instrument squeaked and changed direction, regretting ever getting involved.

"Here!" she said, throwing the crown at him. "You have it!"

He hadn't expected her to go that far, and he flubbed the catch with his shield arm, flicking the crown up into the air and twisting in midstep to turn and try again. Instead, his left toe caught on a lip of stone, and he fell, spread-eagled. The crown came down, striking him on the head — where it stayed.

"Odo?" cried Eleanor.

Shakily, he sat up.

Everyone was looking at him.

Everything was suddenly quiet.

He raised his hands. Yes, the crown was definitely on his head, which, according to the dragon, made him . . .

King of Tofte.

TWENTY-FIVE

All eyes were on Odo. *King* Odo, thought Eleanor in amazement. She couldn't believe it. Who could have guessed when they found Biter in the mud that his journey would lead him here?

Jealousy, this time, was the furthest thing from her mind. She felt only pride for her friend, who she thought would make a very good king indeed.

Lord Deor was the first to recover from the shock. He launched a surprise attack against Hundred, and she blocked too late. Her curved sword spun far out of her reach.

Empty-handed, she stood facing him, apparently helpless. He laughed, gloating, and drew back his sword to strike her down.

She launched herself under the blade, which swung harmlessly overhead. Using her weight in exactly the right way, she tipped him off balance, forcing him back one step, two steps . . .

Lord Deor took no third step. With a cry, he fell into a fiery crack and disappeared. There came a sound like giant jaws crunching, and he was gone.

Out of the crack shot a black streak.

"The falconstone!" cried Biter, instinctively going to follow.

But as the Butcher Blade of Winterset rocketed off into the distance, heading south and west away from the sun, Biter stayed his flight. His knight needed him. The *king* needed him. Perhaps to slay the dragon, if it chose to stir again.

Odo barely noticed. His thoughts were a whirl — but he knew what he had to do. Although being a knight was something he had learned to like, he knew he still had a great deal to learn. Being a king was an even tougher job than being a knight, and he simply wasn't ready for such a task. He was a boy from a village who knew right from wrong, and liked knowing what he was supposed to do. He didn't have the first idea of how to rule an entire country.

Eleanor saw all this pass across her friend's face, and understood completely. She would have done the same in his shoes, but for different reasons. She wanted to see the world, and kings mostly stayed at home and argued with people who wanted things from them. That sounded about as much fun as helping her father lance Old Master Croft's boils.

She could have cheered when he lifted the crown off his head.

"No," he said. "I am not ready to be a king. Perhaps I never will be."

"I'll make you the richest man in Tofte," said Odelyn, sensing victory nearing once more, even though she stood alone among enemies. This knight was just a boy, and boys were easily convinced to act against their better interests. "You'll marry the prettiest woman in Winterset."

"I don't want that either," he said without hesitation. "And besides, it's not my place to choose."

He tossed the crown to Egda, who heard the rush of air and caught it expertly.

"It's a wise man who knows his limitations, Sir Odo," he said, weighing the crown in his hands. He laughed softly. "As I believe I now know mine. I didn't give up the throne because I was blind. I abdicated because I no longer had the desire to rule. I was tired, frustrated, and . . ." He forced himself to utter the word he had resisted for so long. ". . . *old*. But there is no shame in that, just as there is no shame in being blind. I accept the truth now, and tell you with all honesty that I still don't want to be king."

He laughed again, more loudly. "And judging by the quaking underfoot, I suspect the great Aldewrath doesn't want me to be king either!"

Egda paused for a moment, everyone watching, everyone listening.

"But I do know someone who I think is suitable," he continued. "Someone whose clever planning, patience, and humility shows he is fit to be king."

There was complete silence for a moment. Egda raised the crown and said the name.

"Kendryk."

Kendryk slowly walked over to Egda, placed his hands on the old king's shoulders, and knelt before him. Egda lowered the crown on his head. Just as it settled there,

Odelyn made a sudden lunge, only to be prevented by Eleanor and Runnel.

"There," Egda said, tapping the crown lightly on top to make it sit securely. "By the will of the dragon, it is done."

As Kendryk stood up, Egda went down on one knee, and so did Hundred and Odo. Eleanor stayed standing, but only because she didn't trust Odelyn not to run at Kendryk again.

"I might have the crown," said King Kendryk as the rumbles of protest subsided, "but I'm still only a pretender. Our whole family are pretenders!"

"All kings are pretenders," came a rumbling voice from below, and the dragon's head rose out of the rift again. "All *human* kings . . ."

"No!" shrieked Odelyn. She ducked under Eleanor's grasping hands, dodged Runnel's sudden swipe, and ran at Kendryk, only to be caught and wrapped several times around by Aldewrath's lightning-fast tongue. The dragon held her like that for a few seconds, then whipped his tongue back, sending the regent spinning dizzily away until she fell over a stone and lay there, sobbing angrily.

Kendryk looked around in amazement, taking in his great-uncle, grandmother, three knights, and a dragon, all looking at him at once, the only person standing on Old Dragon Stone.

This was his moment, he told himself, after everything he had worked for during his long imprisonment at the hands of the regent, seeking a peaceful way to stop her from becoming king, pretending to be mad so she wouldn't think him a threat. Still, Kendryk had never dreamed that he himself might end up on the throne. That, surely, would fall to someone of the right bloodline. Yet here he was, the start of a *new* bloodline . . .

There was so much to think about.

He lengthened his spine, raised his chin, adjusted the crown so it sat straight across his forehead, and said, "Are you proposing a new pact, great Aldewrath?"

"A modification of the original pact," said the dragon. "This time I will be wary of sorcerers desiring me to sleep overlong."

Kendryk bowed, holding the crown with one hand so it didn't fall off. There had been too much kicking around of that crown already, and he could see several of the gems that had fallen off lying on the ground.

"On behalf of . . . of my people, I apologize for the actions of Brandar the decidedly un-Wise and the forget-fulness of Tofte. It will never happen again."

"I sincerely hope not. Not too often, anyway. I like my sleep, but waking has its pleasures too. The dawn in particular. I will dream of this one while I await the next."

Aldewrath's glassy eyelids flickered and he began to sink back into Old Dragon Stone.

Eleanor's breath caught in her throat. She had a question, but did she dare ask it? Only the thought that she might never get another chance forced her to try.

"Excuse me, Aldewrath?"

The dragon stopped, his snout just visible.

"Harrumph. Yes, little knight?"

"The person who started the pact between humans and dragons — was that the First King?"

"Between all humans and all dragons? I cannot answer that question. But between me and the people of Tofte, it was indeed her. Now, she truly had fire in her veins . . . and many exhausting questions of her own. Good night, and good-bye."

Aldewrath's eyes closed and he disappeared for good. Old Dragon Stone grew silent and still. The cracks healed up. The fires went out. With a steely hiss, the Royal Sword slid out of the rock as though pushed from the inside, and fell flat with a clatter.

King Kendryk gingerly picked it up in his right hand, but it wasn't hot at all. He raised his left hand for Tip to land on, and then transferred the bat to his shoulder. The little bat settled gratefully there, closing his eyes and falling almost instantly asleep. It had been a long night's work, with many surprises. What happened during the daytime was the humans' responsibility.

"Please, stand," said the king. "Sir Odo, Sir Eleanor — I feel as though I already know you from Tip's testimony. You have served my great-uncle well, and by serving him, served me and Tofte as faithfully as any royal guard."

"It was our duty," said Odo.

"And a pleasure," added Eleanor.

"My gratitude is undying and . . . well, I don't know the proper words, but I'm sure I'll find them some day. Let us call your apprenticeship complete, shall we? I pronounce you the first members of the re-formed royal guard. Which means, unfortunately for you, there's still much work to be done. We need to tend the wounded and bind the unrepentant, starting with my grandmother."

Odo bowed and went to fetch the rope they had used to climb the Stone.

Kendryk continued. "Hundred, I believe there are loyal knights in the city. Could you gather them to attend me?"

"Yes, sire. I know three at least who will be eager to serve." She hurried off to summon Sirs Brude, Uen, and Talorc, who were certain to have made short work of the Instruments at the river gate.

"Great-Uncle?"

Egda approached Kendryk, using his staff for support. He knelt before his great-nephew and bowed his head. "I doubt you have any need for a blind, old fool, but whatever I have to offer is yours."

"You *are* a fool if you think I don't need your help." The younger man beamed, even though Egda couldn't see it. "Good kings have good advisers. Perhaps you will be mine, until the kingdom is secure once more?"

Egda bowed. "It would be an honor, sire."

"A madman and a fool in league?" scoffed Odelyn. "I will laugh at you when things fall apart."

"I hardly think that is going to happen, Grandmother," Kendryk said as Odo finished tying her wrists together. "Not while I have such loyal knights and swords at my side."

Odo expected Biter to launch forth in an enthusiastic salute, but none came. The sword's tip kept nudging in the direction the Falconstone had fled, and Odo knew what preoccupied him.

Bowing to accept the compliment, Odo joined Eleanor in checking to see which of the Instruments had woken, and which of those had experienced a sudden and unexpected change of heart.

I still don't understand how you talked Kendryk into letting us go home," said Odo two weeks later.

Eleanor and Odo were in the royal stables, seeing to their horses. Wiggy had arrived several days before from Kyles Frost, along with Eleanor's favorite mount — Belbis, a strawberry roan with a distinct snowcap blanket on her croup and fierce curiosity for everything that lay off the beaten path. In that, she very much reminded Odo of her rider.

"I didn't," said Eleanor in surprise. "I thought you must have done."

"No," said Odo. He scratched his head. "I did say I'd like to go back to Lenburh to see my family sometime . . ."

"I sort of feel we . . . I . . . might have disappointed him," said Eleanor. "And now he's getting rid of us."

"What? No . . . I don't think so," said Odo. "You mean because of what you did to Lady Scrift?"

"Lady Scrift said we were the real rebels and traitors and should have our heads chopped off! Besides, I wasn't going to hurt her. If she'd stayed still she'd never have broken her leg."

"Kendryk . . . the king . . . told me she deserved everything she got," said Odo firmly.

Eleanor sighed as she brushed Belbis down. "I guess I'm just not suited to seeing wrongdoers get away with things. Lady Scrift *volunteered* to be an Instrument."

Odo had nothing to say to that. Though the regent herself had been decreed a traitor, and would spend the rest of her days in Winterset's highest prison cell, Kendryk had pardoned most of the Instruments, Adjustors, and Regulators, though they would all be replaced.

"They should have all been locked up," said Eleanor. "Or had their heads chopped off."

"I think the king was right to be merciful," said Odo. "And I do not think he was worried about you scaring Lady Scrift. He's not sending us into exile or anything."

"No," said a familiar voice from the stable door.

It was Egda, and Hundred was with him. Odo and Eleanor put their brushes aside and hurried to greet their friends. They had hardly seen one another since the coronation, what with exploring the city and learning their duties as royal guards, while Hundred and Egda had been often closeted with the king, offering advice.

"Where have you been?" Eleanor demanded. "I haven't seen you since the feast three days ago."

Odo nudged her warningly. "There's been a lot to do, I bet."

"Indeed," said Egda, but not without an affectionate smile. "Some of the Instruments have disobeyed the instruction to return to the capital, the pardon notwithstanding. Not all the former stewards have been located, nor knights who held other important posts. And we have only just set in train the Great Reckoning, the census that will keep many of those former Instruments busy, as we count and record all the people, holdings, and other minutiae of the kingdom. Kendryk intends to rule with knowledge, not force."

"As befits a sorcerer-king of the first rank," said Hundred. "I believe a ballad is already circulating through the taverns. It also names two young heroes with a bright future ahead of them."

Eleanor blushed with a mixture of delight, embarrassment, and frustration.

"If our future is so bright," she said, "why is the king sending us home now?"

"He knows you are too valuable to waste your time standing guard outside the throne room, or pacing the sentry-walk of the palace," said Egda. "Though I daresay you will have your turns at that in the future."

"But why send us home?" asked Odo. On the one hand, he dearly wanted to see Lenburh again, but on the other it did seem surprising the king wanted them to go. Part of him wondered if it was a mistake and they'd be called back, just when he was starting to think about home again, and the way the river burbled beneath the mill wheel, and the birds sang in the morning . . .

"Hard to say," said Hundred. "There are many such decisions for the king to make."

"Oh," said Eleanor, unable to hide her disappointment. "It just seems, I don't know, odd."

"You thought being a knight was going to be one long adventure?" Hundred asked. She looked at Egda, who smiled. Even though he couldn't see the smile on Hundred's face, he must have heard it in her voice.

"What?" asked Eleanor.

"We must return to the king's side, but before we do, I just want to say what a pleasure it has been serving with you both," said Egda. He was still smiling. "The new ballad does not lie. The future of Tofte is in good hands."

Both of them blushed at the former king's praise, but Eleanor frowned as well. There was something else going on here. Odo also sensed it, and looked at her in puzzlement.

"Oh," Egda said on the threshold. "A word of warning. We have received reports of a renegade sword heading west — an enchanted sword that slays anyone who approaches. Fortunately, the king is sending two of his best knights to deal with it, while on their way to Lenburh."

With that, he and Hundred were gone, and Biter was suddenly out of his scabbard and hissing about the barn, startling the horses.

"A renegade sword?" he cried. "Slaying people? It has to be the falconstone. It must be stopped! We must join forces with these knights."

Odo started to laugh, soon joined by Eleanor.

"What?!" shrieked Biter. "There is not a moment to be lost. We cannot allow these other knights to vanquish our foe!"

"Biter," said Odo, quelling his laughter with difficulty. "We are those knights."

"Oh," said Biter. Odo held out his hand, and Biter returned to it.

"You had better practice your moves, little brother,"

said Runnel, leaping into Eleanor's hand. "*I believe you may still be a little rusty.*"

"*Never!*"

Joining the swords in the joyous playfight, Eleanor and Odo danced back and forth through the sawdust and straw. Whether the future was in good hands or not, they couldn't say, but they could at least feel that it was mapped out with some degree of certainty. One magic sword wouldn't stand a chance against two, not to mention their knights . . .

Could it?

EPILOGUE

Without breaking step, the lone traveler stared up at the mountains in exhausted resignation. She had reached the flanks of the Offersittan and knew what lay ahead: a long and dangerous climb. Already haggard and thin after weeks of walking, clad only in filthy quilted gambeson and hose, she doubted she would live to see the other side. But she had no choice. She had to continue.

"Help! Save me!"

The desperate cry came from over a low hill directly ahead. Unhesitatingly, the traveler started to run. She was going that way anyway, and helping a stranger in need could bring her a meal, perhaps even shelter for the night. She was allowed to rest at night.

What she saw brought her very nearly to a halt. A bearded peasant armed only with a pitchfork was fending off a sword that chopped and slashed entirely of its own volition. An *enchanted* sword!

The traveler hissed through her teeth. Now this was a predicament. She had experience with such swords, recent experience. She knew how deadly they could be.

Even as she approached, the sword lunged, killing the peasant with a single stab to the throat.

The traveler slowed, though she could not stop. This was an even more dangerous sword than she had supposed. Enchanted swords did not usually act without a wielder, and they did not kill peasants.

The sword withdrew from the body and turned in the air towards her, taking the measure of this new arrival. The traveler noted that it had an empty setting where a gem once might have been. It was strange, too, that it did not speak. Maybe it had nothing to say.

"Let me pass," she told the bloodied weapon, her mouth curled. "Or slay me. I care not. I am cursed by a dragon, and must walk on."

The sword answered, but not in speech. It came straight at her, and the traveler forced herself to keep her eyes open, to brace for the killing blow. No one could say she had died like a coward, with her eyes shut.

But at the last second, the sword spun in the air, and the heavy pommel struck her a powerful blow directly above her heart.

She gasped, thrown backward to the ground as though the earth had been pulled out from under her. A terrible pressure spread from the left side of her chest, down her left arm, and up her throat. The sword had stopped her heart! With a single blow! Blackness crept in around the edges of her vision, and she hissed out a curse, unable to do more than feel an incredible wave of anger and futility at dying like this, so pointlessly, and without enacting a terrible revenge on those who had wronged her . . .

The world turned to black. She felt herself rushing down a tunnel as long as a dragon's throat . . .

And then she felt a second blow to her chest that brought her back to life. She drew in a ragged breath, feeling her heart resume beating with a lurch, then a stagger, then a furious racing, driven by panic and relief.

Her vision returned. The sword was hanging over her, mute and deadly.

It had brought her back from the dead!

Why?

An even stranger discovery awaited her on groaning to her feet, her treacherous feet that were condemned to walk east one thousand days. She had endured the dragon's curse barely one-tenth that time, but now . . . now her feet were still.

Experimentally, rubbing her bruised chest, she took a step to her left, then her right, then behind her, away from the mountains. Nothing impeded her.

She could walk anywhere she wanted!

The sword watched her deliberations with patience and, she sensed, no small sense of expectation.

It had broken the curse. She had no doubt of that. By killing her and then restoring her to life, it had freed her from a fate worse than death for any knight, false or otherwise. Humiliation had once been her only destination. But now . . .

Now she had other prospects.

The sword was still watching her. She had no doubt that it could kill her again, in a moment, if it chose.

Furthermore, she supposed the sword would kill her the moment she outlived her usefulness to it, whatever that might be.

She would be sure, in all things, not to give it reason to.

She went down on one knee.

"I am Sir Saskia," she told it, "at your service."

ABOUT THE AUTHORS

Garth Nix and Sean Williams first collaborated on the Troubletwisters series, which they followed with a book in the Spirit Animals series, *Blood Ties*. Garth is also the bestselling author of the Seventh Tower series, the Keys to the Kingdom series, the Old Kingdom series, and *Frogkisser!* Sean's bestselling novels include those in the Twinmaker series and several in the Star Wars® universe. Both Garth and Sean live in Australia — Garth in Sydney and Sean in Adelaide. *Have Sword, Will Travel* was their first book featuring Odo, Eleanor, Biter, and Runnel.